Expressions
of a
Self-Rising Flower

B.L. Gordon

Order this book online at www.trafford.com
or email orders@trafford.com

Most Trafford titles are also available at major online book retailers.

Printed in the United States of America.

ISBN: 978-1-4669-0904-5 (sc)
ISBN: 978-1-4669-0906-9 (hc)
ISBN: 978-1-4669-0905-2 (e)

Library of Congress Control Number: 2011963028

Trafford rev. 12/29/2011

 www.trafford.com

North America & international
toll-free: 1 888 232 4444 (USA & Canada)
phone: 250 383 6864 ✦ fax: 812 355 4082

Looking out over the horizon, I saw the sunlight flirting with the ocean's seemingly calm waters. Then the peaks of the waves started dancing and suddenly there appeared the riotous colors. I was truly mesmerized. This was more awesome than a rainbow. The colors actually came to life. They were dancing and prancing, even laughing and shouting. Those riotous colors were full of movement, full of life. Whoever heard of such a thing? They intermingled and then separated. I even think they winked at me. Those riotous colors are the highlight of the twilight and they only appear once in your life time on the eve of your good night which is your golden hour.

The casket had already been lowered into the freshly dug and now very muddy grave. The black and white United Cab went slowly through the open rusty iron gates of the only cemetery in town at the end of Jackson Avenue. The unexpected heavy summer shower had ended just as soon as it had started. The sunshine made the wet grass and trees glisten in stark contrast to the five remaining people at the gravesite. Marigold found herself shivering despite the warmth of the sun as she hurriedly got out of the cab. At first, she thought the few remaining people at the grave were all strangers. As the distance narrowed with her anxious approach, she could more readily discern faces.

"Darn those flight cancellations," Marigold thought. At least she had visited Uncle Yetis a month ago and he had told her not to worry about him. He had shared with her that the only thing that was puzzling him about dying was the fact that he only had colon cancer instead of liver cancer and kidney failure considering his long history of drinking. Now, at the age of eighty-two he figured he had lived long enough and had beaten the odds in view of his track record. What he wanted to do now was be released from the hospital to go home and let Soya fuss over him. He figured he had already over stayed his welcome on this earth. He also humorously shared with Marigold that he thought life and death were both greedy for his soul. And, at this stage in his life, he was just being tossed backward and forward. It was just a matter of which one would he eventually hold on to the tightest.

Goldie, as Uncle Yetis affectionately called Marigold, was remembering with a smile as she made the flight back home how her uncle could always make her feel better. He had insisted that she take the job that she currently had. Her break-up with Bomar had left her physically, emotionally, and mentally drained. Her uncle had told her that she had too much living to do. There was so much more to life that she needed to explore before she allowed herself to be buried in the small town atmosphere, especially since she was running away from her true feelings. Often he would tell her, "You are like a little seedling, Goldie. You have only sprouted up. You are not full bloom. You need to explore life and be about the business of growing. You are letting your occasional life dramas drain your energy. Just learn the lesson of the moment and move on with your life. You are in control. If I had known at your age what I know now, my life would have been completely different. But it really does not matter how old you are when it comes to understanding your life. The point is that you must come to a truthful understanding. Some people never reach that plateau. Life is really quite simple. Do not make it more complicated. I just want you to be happy."

The flight home to attend the funeral made her reflect on her life, especially since she had moved away from Harahan. She thought about how she finally convinced herself that Uncle Yetis was right. She was able to muster up the courage to leave Harahan. She decided that she was going to make the most of her transition to her new job. She was remembering her first day. She had enjoyed the flight. She was anxious to find herself an apartment. She had two weeks to do that. The company was setting her up in a rather prestigious hotel until she accomplished this. She did not like staying alone in hotels more than three or four nights. She realized the way she was beginning to plan her life she might be alone for a long time. As soon as she had located her luggage, her cell phone rung. She was actually surprised. She was trying to find the exit to locate a cab to escort her to the hotel. The voice on the other end identified himself as Napoleon. He told her that he was driving to the passenger pick up station. He said he would be in a black company Jaguar and for her to give him less than five minutes to pull up. She quickly located the passenger pick up exit. She had to go down to the 1st level. As she stepped out of the exit doors, she immediately spotted the Jaguar to her left. Napoleon pulled up in front of her, put the car in park and hurried out of the car to assist her with her luggage. She only had two suitcases, a matching overnight bag and her shoulder purse. Napoleon quickly assisted her with getting all the luggage in the trunk.

It was a pleasant 86 degrees. Napoleon was dressed casually in a brown leather loafer shoe style without socks. Goldie noticed he also had on stylish designer jeans, a button down front long sleeve light blue shirt opened at the neck. Goldie found herself thinking about Bomar. She felt Napoleon's style of dress would have looked just as flattering on Bomar. Suddenly, Goldie realized that Napoleon was speaking to her. She hoped he had not noticed that for a moment she was preoccupied with her own thoughts. She wanted to appear to be very attentive and make a very favourable first impression.

"Little Lady, Napoleon said in a very amicable manner. "Now that we have your luggage out of the way, let me formerly introduce myself. My name is Napoleon Hart. Here is my company ID card. You must keep that card with you at all times. I am what they call at Vaccarro Del Bell the "COG". That stands for the company's "chief official greeter". I meet all new employees who arrive by plane or train. I make sure that your move here is as smooth and as pleasant as possible. If you need, want, or desire something, then I am the one to bring it about or make it happen for you. I am at your beck and call 24/7 for the first two weeks of your transition. I must admit that your needs seem to be very minimal and very predictable. You have no furniture, no car, no spouse, no children, and you have arrived with only two suitcases and an overnight bag. You must be in a big hurry to leave the past behind. And you are so young to have some relationship baggage. Excuse me! I'm already in your business. But I must confess that I have developed an eye for knowing the signs for needing an immediate change in your life. You must forgive me, but I can assure you that I am not being nosy. I've been doing this job for the last 15 years. I can say with confidence that I am getting better and better everyday. I can also determine from day one who will be staying and who will be leaving Vaccarro Del Bell in a few months."

Goldie avoided eye contact with Napoleon. She hoped she did not appear to be aloof. She was actually amused by and fascinated with him. She was glad that he was very talkative. She had little to say. She always felt that she could be easily read by certain individuals at times. She managed a nervous smile. She dared not ask Napoleon what he had concluded already about her future with Vaccarro Del Bell. She decided she would just have a wait and see attitude. Besides, she had promised Uncle Yetis that she would give this job her best before returning home. That meant she had a fighting chance. She was petite in stature and young, but she knew that she could do the job that she was hired to do if given a chance. She concluded that she did not find Napoleon to be intimidating, but intriguing.

As though reading her mind, Napoleon informed Goldie with a buoyant smile as they exited the airport to travel the brief commute to the hotel that she had a very impressive resume. "As a matter of fact, young lady, I have your complete dossier file in the briefcase on the back seat. I must confess that you are more attractive than the photo in your file. You also look younger. I want you to change out of that stuffy corporate looking pantsuit before I pick you up for lunch at 11:45 a.m. sharp. Your team members will be meeting us for lunch. The dress code is formal/casual. I hope that makes sense to you. One aspect of my job will require that I take you shopping for a wardrobe that fit's the company's image. You have a $5000 clothing allowance to get you started. Your first week here will entail introducing you to every division of the company and make sure you understand what is expected of you as an employee of Vaccarro Del Bell. You will soon realize that being an employee of Vaccarro Del Bell, VDB for short, incorporates every aspect of your life. Exemplary employees who live an open and exemplary life are what we are about. That does not equate to perfection. But the company's founder and owner believes strongly in rewarding honesty, creativity and a giving spirit. You have joined forces with an employer that believes work should be an enjoyable experience. This company believes that we are in a constant state of evolving. So keep an open mind. I feel positive vibrations from you. I assure you that your energy level at VDB will soar. I do love my job. Tomorrow I will pick you up in the morning to start looking for an apartment and a new car. Life can be so exciting and adventuresome. Open yourself up to the limitless possibilities."

Goldie was trying to decide if Napoleon was trying to reassure her or just making conversation. She decided what he was sharing with her made sense. Also, she had concluded that he was a genuine person and one to be trusted. As a matter of fact, she felt very relaxed in his presence. She could tell he was not only well groomed but very intelligent and definitely discerning. She wanted to get to know him better. She felt attracted to him, but she was not enamoured by him. She wondered how old he was. He had a very youthful, but rather mature appearance about him. He was as Uncle Yetis would say, "A young feisty puppy with an old man's eyes."

Again, as though reading her thoughts, Napoleon revealed his age to Goldie.

"Yesterday was my 45th birthday. And you know, since I started working for VDB, I feel that I am not only getting better and better, but more and more youthful as well. The company threw me a big surprise party at the Vaccarro Bella Restaurant last night. It was a blast. I love being happy, don't you?"

Goldie thought that was a strange question to ask.

"Of course, Napoleon, why do you ask?" Goldie responded disconcertedly.

"That was a rhetorical question my dear," Napoleon responded. "Oh by the way, I just love those shoes that you have on. My mother is petite like you. I think that is a good style for me to get her. Oh, it looks like we are here at the hotel. Doesn't time fly by fast when you are having good honest conversation? I will escort you to your room. Your luggage will be brought up. I already have the key to your room with me."

Napoleon got out from the driver's side and rushed to open the door for Goldie. He then put her right arm in his left arm and escorted her inside the hotel like a proud suitor. The car remained parked out front.

"And for your information," Napoleon said in a very proud manner, "this hotel is own and operated by VDB. You are going to be treated like a little princess the two weeks that you stay here. I will make sure that company surrounds you every night. The food is excellent. Your meals are also on the company."

Entering the lobby, Goldie was astounded. It was as though they were walking outdoors instead of going inside a building.

"It's beautiful." was all she could say.

"Doesn't it just energize you?" Napoleon asked. "I have an affinity for nature. Its sights can be so breathtaking. I am especially fascinated with what man's creativity allows him to do, especially when he attempts to imitate nature."

Goldie was speechless as she allowed her eyes to take in the view of the entire lobby area. From the waterfall on the east wall, to the awesome display of flowers and greenery and yes even trees, she was totally captivated. She loved the lighting displays. There was even a rainbow that was so real it appeared to be enchanting. She was trying to absorb it all as Napoleon directed her toward the glass elevators. As they went up to her floor, she could see a more panoramic view of the lobby areas. Napoleon did not speak during the entire ride. Once the elevator stopped, Napoleon also quietly escorted her to her room. It was as though he was allowing her to fully capture the amazing view of the lobby.

"Here we are in your suite, my dear." Napoleon said, "Enjoy and explore. Let me allow the real sunshine in to light up your room. I do not like the curtains drawn during the day. Do you feel that way?"

Since Napoleon was opening the curtains as he spoke, Goldie decided that was another rhetorical question. She smiled at Napoleon and said, "Thank you."

"I will leave you now to get ready for lunch. Remember to call me if you need me, Goldie. Do not hesitate. That means morning, noon, or night my little flower. They pay me well for what I do."

Napoleon was out of the room before Goldie had a chance to make another comment. She had been so busy taking in the full view of what she considered very lavish surroundings that she did not notice him heading for the door.

She felt herself feeling overwhelmed by the extravagant design of her suite. It was just as impressive to her as the lobby. She kept opening and closing her eyes momentarily and telling herself she must be dreaming. She decided she must call her aunt and uncle.

"Aunt Soya, I enjoyed the two hour flight and I am enjoying my hotel." Goldie said in a jubilant voice that pleased her aunt. "I meant to call you when I arrived at the airport."

"It's okay, Goldie," said Aunt Soya. "That nice Mr. Hart called me already and told me that you had a safe arrival. He gave me your hotel information. He sounded like a very nice man. Is he single?"

Goldie was too excited to become annoyed with her aunt regarding her question about Napoleon's marital status. She politely informed her aunt that Napoleon was not married, but he was too old for her. However, she did interject that she found him to be simply adorable and looked forward to getting to know him better. That response seemed to please her aunt.

Is Uncle Yetis home?" Goldie asked. She was very anxious to speak briefly with her uncle.

"No, he isn't." was Aunt Soya's prompt response. "He's out completing some errands. I will let him know as soon as he gets back that you called. Mr. Hart told me he will make sure that you get settled into a nice apartment in a safe neighbourhood. He also mentioned that he was taking you to lunch and dinner today. I am very excited that you will be getting out more. I want you to cooperate with that Mr. Hart. You tell him thanks for calling. I have a good feeling about that man."

Goldie was wondering how the conversation went between Napoleon and her aunt. He certainly had won her over. She was beginning to appreciate Napoleon more and more. She would give him a big thank you when they met again. Now, she must unpack. Afterwards, she decided to freshen up in the bathroom. As she closed the door behind her, she noticed an envelope on the vanity. She picked it up when she realized it was addressed to her. Inside was a greeting card from Napoleon welcoming her to VDB. In addition, there was also a small insert with the company's information, including office and home phone numbers of the company's owner and all of the other employees. There was also a beautiful live floral arrangement sitting on the vanity in a golden vase with a little card attached that read, "Welcome aboard. You are now part of a unique team of value players. We look forward to learning more about you, your skills, and talents. Creatively Yours, Your new family and friends at Vaccarro Del Bell."

Goldie was elated to receive the card and the flowers. The company was doing an excellent job of making her feel like a valued employee. She felt she had a six sense that this was a wise choice on her part. Of course, Uncle Yetis was the motivating factor in her decision to accept her new position. She must talk to him soon. She was missing him. She would call him tonight.

Napoleon returned to the hotel promptly at 11:45 a.m. He called Goldie from the lobby on the guest phone. He was quite pleased that she was ready. He told her that she was stuck with him for the rest of the day. She would have a break after lunch and then he would pick her up at 7 p.m. for dinner.

"We're to meet your team members at The Whistle Blower Restaurant for lunch. It's a fun, hot spot for dinning, live music, and dancing. On Wednesday and Thursday evenings improvisations are the main form of entertainment. Friday nights are also open for the patrons to get up and share information on whatever topics they choose in 5 minutes segments from 8:00 p.m. until 9:30 p.m. It is also owned by our company. It is quite unique for a restaurant. It opens at 6:30 a.m. as a breakfast buffet, then it shuts down at 9:00 a.m. and reopens at 11:30 a.m. for lunch with a carry out and eat in venue. This is to accommodate the many patrons who show up daily. Lunch ends at 2:30 p.m. and they become a night spot at 8:00 p.m. What is interesting is that the wall decorations are like shades that you can pull up and down. You have a morning, noon, and night atmosphere. Mr. Drummaday always said The Whistleblower was about beauty in knowing as we evolve in this simply amazing and wonderful world. You must find enjoyment in life all day long every day. It makes you thankful and grateful and energizes you. It is time for you to remove that dark cloud over your head, Goldie. Remain with Vaccarro Del Bell and you will wake up with a smile on your face and you will be surrounded by joy and laughter. As it has often been said, 'Don't worry. Be happy.' And to add another famous quote to that, 'Worry is a misuse of your imagination.' It has taken me a long time to appreciate the simple truths in life. I can tell now that I have met you that you are going to be an asset to your team at VDB. Mr. Drummaday could tell from your resume' and photo."

Goldie quickly replied, "I am glad to hear that, Napoleon. I trust your judgement. I am definitely at your mercy. I must also add that any one who can win my Aunt Soya over the phone has to be very special. Obviously, you are a man who understands people."

Goldie also felt that Napoleon was a man who was very observant. He was reading her like a book. She was finding him more and more fascinating, but sometimes she felt that he was revealing more than she understood. She was looking forward to being in his company more and more. She had to admit she felt more buoyant in his presence.

Napoleon was glad to see that Goldie was in good spirits. He felt that if he could keep her that way, she would be more relaxed when she met her team members, Randall, Cade and Chloe. They were curious and anxious to meet Goldie. The three also hoped she would be a good mix for the group. They would be working very close together as research auditors which sometimes meant long hours and trips out of town together.

Everyone was seated when Napoleon and Goldie arrived. They had decided to wait on Napoleon and Goldie before ordering their meals. Napoleon took the lead in introducing everybody. His knack for drawing people out was apparent in this small and intimate group setting. It was as though her future team members were following Napoleon's lead.

Napoleon was glad to see how the other's warmed up to Goldie. He also noticed that Randall was especially attentive to her. He just hoped the two would take sometime to get to know each before getting too close. Young love he mused could be so sweet and so opaque. There was a sense of incompleteness about both of them. Why do we tend to want others to make us complete rather than become complete on our own was now an enigma to him. He was glad that needy phase was behind him. He was truly enjoying life for the first time. His break-up with his girlfriend, Ophelia, almost 15 years ago took a toll on him. But thanks to his mother, his two aunts and Mr. Drummaday, he was able to reconnect with his own true essence. Loving someone else should begin with you feeling complete and understanding what you are about in this big vast universe. Most of us will not look closely at ourselves in the mirror because we are afraid of what we might see. He learned that from Mr. Drommaday that two complete souls are empowering, otherwise there is a draining of each other's energy. His love for Ophelia had been filled with constant drama. He realized they were passionately in love, but they were both very demanding of each other. He was also very protective of Ophelia, yet he always felt that she was too invasive of his space. They would try to pull away from each other, only to plunge back into a deeper need to be together. They were total opposites in too many ways. It was obvious they were afraid to let each other go for all of the wrong reasons. In the end, it was Ophelia who got up the strength to leave. He had been completely devastated in the beginning, but in time he regained his strength and his senses as his mother and aunts said. Of course, he began dating after a while, but he was no longer looking for someone to make him whole. His relationships, however, were short term because he had developed an instinct for recognizing when his dates had too much personal drama going on to make a long term commitment. Family and friends were always trying to pair him up with someone. Mr. Drummaday, his mother and aunts seemed to be the only ones to understand. However, his mother and aunts were beginning to get anxious for him to meet someone that was compatible. He would tell them that in due time this significant other would appear. In the meanwhile, he wanted to make sure that he was ready. He was eager to tell his mother and aunts about his "new project" which is how he referred to new employees coming in under him. He was eager for them to meet Goldie. He knew they would just adore her.

As the lunch was ending, Randall informed Napoleon that there was a vacancy in his condo units. Napoleon was thrilled to hear that. He felt it would be good for Goldie to be near a team member. Plus, she could carpool with Randall. The condos were a 20 minute commute by interstate. Randall did mention that there was a waiting list but he felt as an employee of Vaccarro Del Belle, she had a very good chance of getting the condo.

"Tell me, Randall, "Is that lovely Ms. Aleyah Futrell still the residence manager of your condominiums?" Napoleon asked.

"Yes, she is." Randall responded not the least surprised that Napoleon knew her.

"That is just great. I ran into her last week while shopping with my mother at Aurora's. She was the former resident manager at an apartment complex that I lived in several years ago. She's a jewel. She and my mother are planning to attend the Music Festival at Central Gardens this weekend. She told me that she was still in the same line of work, but I did not ask her where. This is just great, Goldie. She's going to just love you. I will call her after lunch. I am sure she will agree to meet with us tomorrow."

Goldie was relieved to think that she might have a neighbor who was also a co-worker. She was also glad that it was Randall. She was very aware of the attention that he was giving her. She was trying to avoid direct eye contact with him. She felt it was just too soon for her to become involve with anyone. She hoped the friendship thing would work for them. Overall, she was enjoying lunch with her new team members. She decided she liked all three of them and hoped they felt the same about her. Of course, she felt Randall was willing to accommodate her.

The drive back to the hotel after lunch was quiet and uneventful. Goldie felt as though Napoleon was in deep thought. Suddenly, he said effusively, "This is just wonderful. I am positive that your team members like you, Goldie. Now, make sure that you are ready again promptly at 6:00 p.m. I have a marvellous evening planned for you and your team members. Do not be afraid to tell me if this seems to be too much for you. If you want to retire for the rest of the day, it is your choice."

Goldie promptly responded with an affirmative nod of the head while smilingly with eager anticipation. Yes, she was somewhat tired. But one thing she was sure of, she sure of; she did not want to be alone her first night in town.

Napoleon was pleased with her ardent response. As he parked in front of the hotel entrance, he reminded her to call him if she needed anything.

"I want you to also keep in mind, Ms. Goldie, a quote that my mother always shared with me starting with my teen years, "There was never a night or a problem that could defeat sunrise or hope." I think a Bern Williams is the author of that wise statement. Anyway, it comes to mind as my day winds down. If I have had a rather trying day, that quote helps me focus on the prospect of having a better tomorrow."

Goldie decided she liked the quote and would keep it in mind as she settled in with VDB and adjusted to being away from her family. She reached over and gave Napoleon a quick hug before exiting the car. She was eager to get back to her beautiful room.

Goldie called Uncle Yetis as soon as she entered her room. Uncle Yetis was relieved to know that her first day had gone quite well. He informed her that Aunt Soya was convinced that she could not be in better hands since she spoke with that wonderful Mr. Napoleon Hart. They both had a good laugh about that.

"Do I have some competition to worry about, Goldie?" Uncle Yetis asked with mocked concerned. I can not recall my wife ever being impressed by someone she has not met in person. I am anxious to have a phone conversation with that Mr. Napoleon as soon as possible."

"I assure you, Uncle Yetis," Goldie said "that he is too young for Aunt Soya, but he is handsome and quite charming. I think that you will be very impressed with him as well after you speak with him. He is already proving to be an anchor for me. I also want you to know that I am very excited about my new team members and my job. Vaccarro Del Belle treats their employees like family. Although this is my first day, I can tell my apprehensiveness has decreased tremendously. I am feeling terrific about accepting this job offer. Thank you so much for encouraging me to accept this opportunity."

"That's absolutely wonderful, sweetheart. Hopefully, this means you will have time for social activities as well as work." Uncle Yetis responded excitedly, but with caution. Goldie was like the daughter he never had. Although, she was very smart and intelligent, she was also sensitive and introverted. He had encouraged her to accept the job offer out of town to broaden her horizon. In addition, he was just as concerned about Goldie as Soya since her break up with Bomar.

"Oh, Uncle Yetis, don't you worry about me too. It feels good to be venturing into new territories. Napoleon will make sure of that."

"Well, I am glad to hear that. Now, I am sure Soya told you to call everyday."

"Yes she did was Goldie's prompt response. She even said I should call morning, noon, and night. It looks like we will be communicating now that I am gone more than when I was home." Goldie chuckled at this thought. "I love you, Uncle Yetis. I will be calling you back as soon as possible."

"I love you too, Baby Girl."

Goldie thought about how she used to hate to be referred to as Baby Girl, but now it sounded comforting to her. The family had latched on to that name because Caleb felt it was time to give the title of being the baby in the family to her. He was thrilled when Goldie arrived and glad to have someone younger than him in the household. As she hung up the phone after speaking with her uncle, she realized she was tired. She stretched out across her very comfortable bed and drifted off to sleep. She was dreaming happy dreams of flying through a wonderland and meeting beautiful people who welcomed her to a new land filled with joy and love; she was a smiling baby.

Goldie was awaken by the hotel phone in her room ringing to the tune of "Sleep Little Baby". It was 5:00 p.m. She was glad for the call. It was her Aunt Soya. She wanted to remind Goldie to thank Mr. Hart for his kindness in helping her to adjust to her new surroundings. Mr. Hart had called back and spoken with Uncle Yetis. They both had decided that he was a very nice man. This amused Goldie. She told her aunt about the plans for the evening. Of course, she should have known that Napoleon had already shared this information with Uncle Yetis. Nevertheless, Goldie enjoyed the pleasantness in her aunt's voice during this call.

Napoleon was prompt again when he picked her up for the dinner date. He had changed into a St. John's Bay plaid shirt with a pastel orange and rusty brown colored background. He wore beige dress trousers. This time he had on tan shoes with tan socks. His belt matched his shoes. Goldie felt that his 6' plus height and slender built made him look very handsome. She was guessing his height based on Bomar's six foot frame. She found herself really checking Napoleon out as she walked toward him. His very dark and thick eyebrows were an impressive contrast to his completely bald scalp. She also liked his mustache. Bomar was with out any facial hairs and had a head full of thick black hair with some grey beginning to show at the sides. She wondered how the two would have gotten along. There she was again, thinking about Bomar.

"You look lovely, my dear." said Napoleon with a very attentive look.

Goldie felt somewhat awkward when she realized Napoleon had been scrutinizing her as much as she had been scrutinizing him. She remained taciturn as she approached him.

Napoleon ignored her silence. "You have very sexy legs, young lady. I was glad to see that you chose to wear a dress tonight. I love to see women in dresses."

Goldie was flattered. She found herself managing a slight smile. She was glad Napoleon approved what she was wearing. She had tried on three outfits before deciding to wear the dress. She decided the high heel sandles and clutch bag were the best choice as well. She had to admit that she thought that she looked good.

"You know, Goldie," Napoleon said as they got in the Jaguar, "I was looking forward to dinner more than lunch. I have already made a call to Ms. Futrell. She said if the vacancy that she has now is to your liking the apartment is yours. That gives us a head start on getting furnishing for you. You will charge all your furnishing on the company's account. Payroll will deduct a reasonable amount from your monthly pay. Believe me, VDB has connections. You will be pleased with the selections, style and cost of your furnishings. I am already sizing you up based on your personality. I believe the starter car for you is the newest Honda Civic. You will select the color. I have already contacted my friend, Shelton, at the dealership. This will be a busy week. We will see Ms. Futrell on tomorrow morning after breakfast. You can do what you like for lunch. I will pick you up at 3 p.m. to visit the car dealership. We will meet for dinner again around 7 p.m. with your team members for a fun evening after you have rested from the day's activities. On Wednesday, we will go furniture shopping and look for household items if you feel up to it, otherwise, we will make a day of it on Thursday. On Friday, I will take you to the office after an 8:00 a.m. breakfast. Of course this schedule is contingent on you liking your condo, which I am certain that you will. I hope to see you moved in and settled by next Tuesday. Wednesday and Thursday will allow you to get things organized at the condo. Your team members will be available to assist. I will make sure everything is delivered timely. I hope you do not feel that I am rushing you, dear friend, but when you get into your work routine, you will find little time for these matters."

Goldie was trying to let everything that Napoleon was telling her sink in. She could tell that he enjoyed what he did and was very proficient at it. She could almost envy Napoleon, but she also thought that he must have some issues. There was a side to him that did perplex her. He seemed to have a strong sense of drive about keeping busy. He was always planning ahead, as though being afraid to slow down.

"I guess you are probably somewhat curious about me, Goldie." Napoleon said for the second time that day as though reading her mind.

Again, Goldie felt herself being speechless. It was uncanny to her how Napoleon could sense her concerns. He was clearly insightful and very observant of her.

"You know, Goldie," he continued on as though oblivious to her reaction, "life is truly about choices. When my precious Ophelia left me, I felt like my world had come to an end. As a matter of fact, I felt like the whole world should come to an end. How could life continue on without Napoleon and Ophelia? We were meant to be forever. How could the sun continue to shine? How could the birds continue to fly and make the beautiful chirping sounds that Ophelia and I loved? How could the beautiful flowering trees and plants continue to bloom? How could she continue to smile at me in all of the photos that I had of her? How could she ever leave me for someone else? I am sure you get the big picture by now. I was pathetic."

"Napoleon, I can not imagine any woman leaving you just from what I have observed." Goldie spoke those words with such strong conviction that Napoleon decided he might have been too melodramatic in revisiting his past momentarily.

"Well, break-ups happen to the best of us, Little Lady. It has been a long journey moving on with my life. Perhaps you have heard the quote "When the student is ready, the teacher will come." Ask me if I learned the lesson of the moment. Loosing Ophelia was actually the best thing that happened to me. I was 25 years old when I met Ophelia and 32 years old when we parted company. Never again will I allow myself to feel so incomplete that I would allow another individual who is as incomplete as me drain me of my energy, my thirst for life, or my quest to be complete. When Ophelia left, I shut down. I actually locked myself in my apartment and refused to leave. I did call my mother and I told her to give me sometime to get myself together. Ater 3 day's of not hearing from me, she showed up at my apartment with my aunts. My mother had called my job and informed them that I was suffering from severe heartburn. There was some validity to that. Mother always believed in half-truths if there is indeed such a thing. I am planning for you to meet my mother and two aunts on Saturday. The three of them raised me from age 4 years after my father drowned in a hotel pool while we were on vacation."

Goldie could tell Napoleon was open to sharing a lot about himself this evening since there would be too many other matters for them to focus on as the week went by. She wondered if he was trying to get to know her more personally, or he just loved talking about himself. She was curious, but she was not prepared for the details. She felt there was a motive that she was not grasping. She decided in time if she remained with VDB, she would probably tell him about Bomar. Currently, she felt that she did not need to be so open on her part at this time. She decided to remain silent and just let Napoleon talk.

"By now, you have probably concluded that I am an only child. I feel that my mother and aunts did an excellent job of raising me. I loved sports and was very involved with them and with their support from the age of ten through high school I was a star athlete. In college, I developed a love for Botany. I departed from sports and became a Botanist much to the relief of the three ladies in my life. I had just completed my Master's in that field when I met Ophelia at the company that hired me. Excuse me for rambling. Anyway, after three days of trying to literally fall asleep in death, my mother and aunts showed up unannounced at my apartment to resurrect me. Fortunately, my mother had keys to my apartment. The three ladies rushed in on me in my bedroom. They open up all the curtains in my apartment. Then they removed the covers off me, causing me to fall on the floor and insisted that I take a shower. If not, they would bring the shower to me. Somehow, I crawled into the bathroom. My mother turned on the shower. I crawled into the shower on my hands and needs and sat on the floor for a few seconds before standing up. In the meanwhile, my aunts found my music collection of Baruch CD's and started playing them so loud, I felt that the tenants might complain to the resident manager. My mother found me something to wear and hung my clothes on the back of the bathroom door. The three ladies threaten me by insisting that if I was not dressed and out of the bathroom in ten minutes, they would dress me themselves."

Suddenly, Goldie felt herself overcome by laughter. She realized what Napoleon was telling her was serious, but with her vivid imagination and his detailed discription of things, how could the listener not see a humorist twist to the compelling story. She tried to focus by looking out of her passenger side window. She sneaked a glance at Napoleon. When she realized he was smiling, she felt less embarrassed by her outburst.

"So, you are finding the story of my recovery from my sweet love to be rather amusing, young lady." Napoleon was obviously faking that he was disappointed in Goldie. "In any event, I will continue. We still have about 20 minutes to get to the restarant. Now, there must be no more interuptions or I will start this story at the beginning with more details that I have intentionally left out."

Goldie momentarily wondered if Napoleon shared this bit of history about his life with any of the other new employees coming on board with VDB. Nevertheless, if his purpose was to make her feel more relaxed and amused, she decided he was doing a fantastic job.

"As I was saying, before being so rudely interrupted, before long those ladies had me drinking hot samurai chai mate tea and homemade flaxseed crackers that they had brought to give me an energy boost. They also forced me out of my apartment and insisted that I climb into the front seat of my mother's Acura truck. They continued playing Baruch music, more softly, as they conversed happily with each other. It was as though I was not in the vehicle with them. It was a hot July day and the sunlight insisted on shinning through the front window into my eyes. Before I realized it, my mother was driving around in a rather upscale neighborhood totally unfamiliar to me, but she seemed to be quite familiar with the area. I was getting ready to insist that one of my aunts sit up front since I did not have on my sunshades. Suddenly, my mother pulled into a very impressive driveway and as she did the gates automatically opened. Mother came to a complete stoop at the edge of the driveway and insisted that I get out and ring the doorbell. I was beginning to feel at the mercy of the three ladies. Like a little child, I managed to get out of the truck and proceeded to the front door. Suddenly the front and back passenger windows went down, my mother and aunts were waving at me and at the same time telling me they looked forward to seeing me soon. And to my chagrin, I realized my mother was also turning around to exit the premises. I actually entertained the thought of running after them; however the front door of the mansion opened. I turned my attention back to the front of the home and there stood Mr. Avis Drummaday wearing a tennis outfit. His first words were "Those girls got away from me again!" Then he said, "You must be Napoleon. I was expecting you. You are just in time to be my tennis partner. The girls told me that you were a very versatile athlete. You obviously have the look and built. Let's go to the guest house and see if I have an outfit your size. Oh by the way, you will be staying here for several days in the guest house. You must eat something before you play. The girls said you should be good and hungry by now. Tomorrow, I will discuss with you the new position that I want to hire you for with my company. Now that I have met you, I can tell you are definitely the one for the job."

"So that is how you ended up at VDB?" Goldie inquired with a very captivated interest by now.

"It certaintly was, my dear. And that was the day that I started being in charge of my life again. Mr. Drummaday took me under his wings, so to speak. My wonderful mother and caring aunts had informed him about my situation after a chance encounter with him at one of his restaurants the first day of my break-up. Do you know they had invited him to dine with them after seeing him eating alone? They had no idea who he was at the time. In any event, he had insisted that they bring me over to his home to meet me. The three asked to make a test run to where he lived, so they could easily find it when they brought me. He had insisted that they come by the next afternoon. Mr. Drummaday is divorced and childless. He is a frequent Sunday guest at my mother's home. He also treats me like a son. He has helped me to appreciate that in life you have two choices, which is to be happy or be sad. If you want good things to happen to you be happy, thankful and giving. He figured that out in his early twenties. You can have or be whatever you want in life. There is no magic formula. A lot of people confuse their own personal dogmas and beliefs with what is truth. Just learn to act and look happy; soon you will feel happy. You will find that it is a great life afterall."

Goldie recalled how Uncle Yetis was always telling her to just smile and act happy. Undoubtedly, she was not trying hard enough. Although, she felt today she had smiled and laugh more genuinely than she had for sometime, especially since her break-up with Bomar. There she goes again. She was beginning to realize, that she had to purge herself of that man. But how do you let go of something that you know deep down inside is not what you honestly want to do. She must explore this inner conflict. Hopefully, being around so much positiveness will bring her a calmer spirit. But for now, she concluded that the truth of the matter was that she was still in love with Bomar. Perhaps, now that she was entirely on her own she would find the self-completeness that has been evading her.

"Now that I have bored you with a condensed version of my life history," Napoleon stated scrupulously as he pulled up into The Whistle Blower Restaurant's parking lot, "I will display much effort to not revert to any more conversation about me for the rest of the evening."

Goldie could tell Napoleon did not want to appear to be officious. She was still excited about seeing her team members again. Napoleon's attempt to feel her out and help her relax was working. She was looking forward to having a private audience with him again. The evening turned out to be just as delightful as lunch. Conversation was flowing. Everyone appeared to be commodious. Goldie felt drawn to her team members. The evening came to an end too soon for her. Napoleon dropped her off at the hotel at 11:15 p.m.

It had been a long first day, but she felt invigorated and was anxious about meeting with Napleon the next day.

"I will pick you up at 9:30 for breakfast." Napoleon informed her as he escorted her to the hotel lobby. "Business casual is the attire for the day. We want to make a favourable impression on Ms. Futrell. I have no doubt that she will be pleased to meet you."

The two weeks that were allowed for Goldie to make her transition went by faster than she had realized. Napoleon kept her busy wrapping things up as far as her living arrangements were concerned. She was able to have a busy social life as well. Her new team members invited her out on several occasions without Napoleon. She was able to get some sight seeing done. She sent souvenirs to her aunt and uncle. She was able to meet Napoleon's mother, Adair and two Aunts, Callie and Jodie. They were charming, delightful and very entertaining. She was also able to meet with Mr. Drummaday the second Friday in his office. Despite numerous phone call interuptions, he managed to personally welcome her and informed her of his open door policy. It pleased her that he was quite personable. He was also a very handsome 55 years old gentleman who Goldie felt could have easily passed for 45 years of age.

Goldie's first two years at VDP were rather uneventful, but Goldie loved every waking moment of being part of the very prosperous company. Mr. Drummaday was a true visionary. He was also a man of many talents. He operated VDB like a proud father. He had several projects going on at the same time. His sense of organization and timing were remarkable. At times he appeared to be cogent in the operation of his company, but Goldie detected an altruistic spirit about him that seemed to draw others to him. His employees were very productive and he was very generous in rewarding them for their creativity and honesty as Napoleon had initially informed her. Christmas and Thanksgiving bonuses and annual raises were very important to Mr. Drummaday. The entire operation closed for one week in November and December. In addition, employees were given an entire day off on the anniversary of their hire date. Vacation was two weeks annually. Those with two or more years with the company received a bonus vacation pay check. Some of the business operations were over seas and there were extra incentives for employees who accepted these positions.

Goldie and her team members were proving to be a valuable asset to the company. They just seem to click together as Mr. Drummaday felt that they would. Their ability to catch forgeries had saved the company millions of dollars in unnecessary art acquisitions. Goldie was fascinated with Randall's adroit talent for this. He was a natural as far as she was concerned. The other's mostly relied on extensive research. And usually when Raymond had his suspicions, he was right on the mark. Her respect for him excited Randall. After two years, he finally approached Goldie about seriously dating.

By now, Goldie had grown very close to Napoleon. The relationship remained platonic. When Randall had approached her about dating, she decided to talk it over with Napoleon. She should have realized by now what his response would be.

"Does it make you happy to be with Randall, Goldie?" was his initial response.

"Of course!" was her prompt reply.

"Then, why are we having this conversation, my little flower? I think it is very apparent to everyone that you make Randall happy. Only you know if Randall actually makes you happy. What more can I say?"

Despite the passing of time and a close personal friendsip, Goldie still felt that Napoleon had a way of telling her a lot in as few words as possible. Since being at VDB, she had become more confident in her decision making skills. However, she had avoided being involved in a serious relationship since her break-up with Bomar. She was finally able to go several weeks without thinking about him and when she did she did not fee all of the emotional baggage that had previously weighed so heavily on her heart. She felt that Randall would be a good choice at this time to move on with her life. They had so much in common and he had always been very considerate of her. Besides he made her laugh.

Randall was elated when Goldie agreed that they could be officially considered as a couple. VDB did not discouraged employees dating. Several successful and happy marriages were now part of the company's history. Couples were expected to remain strictly professional on the job at all times.

Goldie found being with Randall was more than she had bargained for. He was so kind and patient with her. She grew to bery comfortable with him. His focus was always on making her happy. They vacationed together and Randall took her to Chicago to meet his parents. He was a man of many talents. He could cook, enjoyed tennis and basketball. He was an excellent swimmer and insisted that she learn golfing. He also was a marathon runner. Goldie just took on his interests. The two enjoyed being together. After about eighteen months of dating, Goldie decided things were getting to be very serious between them. She finally informed her uncle and aunt about the relationship. She realized it was time for her to take Randall home to meet her family all though he had never brought it up himself.

Of course, she should have known when she called a few weeks before Thanksgiving to inform Uncle Yetis that she would be bringing someone home to meet him, that Napoleon had kept him informed since the beginning of her relationship with Randall. Fortunately, it had all been good news.

"We were wondering when we would have the opportunity to meet the young man. You have been home only once since you moved away. You only stayed three days." Aunt Soya's curiosity to meet Randall was very apparent. "I was beginning to think that Yetis and I needed to get on a plane and simply show up on our own to meet this mysterious man in your life."

Actually, Goldie decided that would be a good idea. She dreaded going home and she thought a trip out of town would be good for her aunt and uncle.

"Aunt Soya, I have decided to take you up on that offer. You and Uncle Yetis are going to fly here this weekend. I will not take no for an answer. You'll finally get a chance to meet Napoleon in person as well."

Goldie knew the opportunity to meet Napoleon would make this an offer that her aunt and uncle would not refuse. She could not wait to inform Napoleon. She was glad that it was Monday night. She wanted her aunt and uncle to arrive on Thursday. They could return home by flight on Sunday night. She knew Randall would be delighted to finally meet them. She was becoming more and more excited. She wondered why she had not considered this plan earlier. Neither her aunt, nor her uncle had been on a plane and they seldom travelled out of town except to attend funerals, or an occasional family reunion. This would be a wonderful experience for them since she was going to pay for the entire trip. They could stay with her in the extra bedroom that she had never used for company.

On Thursday, at 06:30 p.m., Napoleon and Randall met Uncle Yetis and Aunt Soya at the airport to their surprise. Aunt Soya was very delighted to meet Napoleon in person and wondered why her niece did not establish a more personal relationship with him. She found Randall to be quite handsome, but she was not immediately drawn to him. She decided that she and her niece must talk alone before her return trip back home. As fas she was concerned, Napoleon had a youthful, fun and entertaining side to him that overshadowed the age difference.

Uncle Yetis was impressed with Napoleon and Randall. He felt his niece could not have paired up with two more sensible and caring men. The ride to Goldie's condo was filled with flowing conversation. Randall was driving and was trying to pass by some tourist sights on the way. Soya was enjoying herself and was being shown a lot of attention by Napoleon and Randall. Uncle Yetis appreciated that. He had never seen her so excited about taking a trip. Their sons, Caleb and Greer, could not believe the two of them had agreed to make the trip by plane. Caleb had called Goldie to confirm that it was true.

Goldie had a wonderful dinner prepared when they arrived. Randall and Napoleon had done their share to help make it a success. Napoleon's mother had made a banana pudding and a chicken cacciatore dish. His aunts had contributed salmon crumb casserole. Goldie had also invited Cade and Chloe.

For Goldie, the real star during her aunt and uncle's visit was her Randall. He was as impressive as Napoleon as far as she was concerned. Aunt Soya was guardedly cordial with him. Nevertheless, Randall made his presence known as he arrived each day to accompany Goldie as she attempted to keep her aunt and uncle preoccupied during their entire stay. He was the chauferr for all the travelling. He even took Uncle Yetis to a local sports bar to give Goldie and her aunt time to be alone. Sunday arrived all too soon for Goldie. She had really enjoyed their visit. Aunt Soya did allow Randall to hug her goodbye at the airport. Uncle Yetis even insisted that Goldie and Randall spend Thanksgiving with them.

Meeting Goldie's aunt and uncle boosted Randle's confidence to ask Goldie to marry him. It had been a month since their visit. He wanted the engagement to be made before their visit with Aunt Soya and Uncle Yetis in November. He planned the engagement over a candlelight dinner at his apartment. Goldie seemed so much more relaxed after her aunt and uncle's visit. He had taken Chloe with him to pick out the ring.

Two weeks before Thanksgiving Randall finally got up the courage to ask Goldie to marry him. The week had been very busy for them at work. He could hardly wait for Friday to come. Goldie had noticed a restlessness about him all day at work. When he informed her that he was leaving two hours early, she thought perhaps he might be ill. However, when he told her that their Friday night date was still on, she decided he just needed some time to rest.

Randall arrived to pick Goldie up at 7:30 p.m. She was looking forward to going out to dinner at a new restaurant that Napoleon had told them about. Randall informed her that he needed to go back to his condo before they went out. She decided to wait in the car for him. However, he insisted that she come inside with him. To Goldie's surprised when they entered the condo, she immediately noticed how beautifully the dinning table was decorated and there was soft romantic music playing. The lights were dimmed. She thought perhaps Randall was trying to convince her to consider moving in with him again. This time she was thinking more seriously about saying yes. Suddenly, he grabbed her in his arms and held her closely. Then he let her go and walked her to the sofa. There was a rather large package the size of a shoe box beautifully wrapped on the coffee table. Randall picked it up and gave it to her as she sat down. He was smiling like a happy little boy. He encouraged her to open it. Her hands were trembling. She could not imagine Randall buying her a pair of shoes and wrapping them up with such care. As she unwrapped the present, Randall jumped up and brought her handbag to her. He told her to check and see if her keys were in her bag. She wondered why he would insist that she stop in the middle of unwrapping the present to check and see if she had her keys. Perhaps this was the way he was leading up to asking her to move in with him. She cooperated and searched her handbag for her keys which were on a key ring. When he asked if she had her car keys, she stated yes. Then he told her to look closer. She held the key chain in front of his eyes to assure him that she was looking at her car keys. Suddenly, she realized another item was on the key ring. She remain momentarily speechless. Then she screamed, "Randall, how did you get possession of my key chain? This ring is . . . . I don't know . . . . !"

Randall removed the keyring from her hand. He then removed the engagement ring and got on his knees. He reached for Goldie's left hand. Before Goldie could say anything, he asked her to marry him. "Goldie, he said with much fervor, I love you with all my heart. Knowing you these past three years has added an excitement to my life that makes me look forward to each new day. I had my eyes on you from the moment you entered The Whistle Blower Restaurant with Napoleon. Your smile was poignant. Your walk was cute and dainty. When you sat down and I was able to occasionally glance into those big round brown eyes, I felt there was nothing otiose about. The passing of the time has only made me love and appreciate you more. Now, I want you to be more than my girlfriend. I want to introduce you as my wife."

Goldie found herself looking intensely into Randall's eyes. Yes, this wonderful and sometimes coy gentleman coveted her. They had never had a bitter moment. "How could she not love him?" she thought.

"Yes, Randall." she said with a longing for him to take her up in his arms and just hold her. Randall grabbed her at that moment and kissed her passionately. He felt her go limp in his embrace. He laid her gently on the couch. Dinner would have to wait.

Goldie could hardly wait to inform Napoleon about her engagement on Sunday evening after Randall dropped her off at home. The two had spent the entire weekend together and she was still basking in the joy of knowing that soon this man would be the prince charming that would be her life long partner. Napoleon had stopped by after failing to reach her by phone. He had also brought some paint colors for Goldie to look at. He was planning to assist his aunts and mother with painting several rooms before the holidays. When Goldie answered the doorbell, he could sense a happiness about her. He concluded she had probably spent the weekend with Randall. He hoped all was moving in the right direction and that Goldie was still in control.

"Napoleon, how do you like my engagement ring?" Goldie said with what could be described as guarded excitement.

Goldie held out her hand for him to see.

Napoleon felt the ring was simply exquisite. Then looking Goldie directly in the eyes, he told her, "Randall is a good man. He deserves the best in life just as you do my dear. I hope you are feeling happy about being happy."

Goldie was disappointed with Naploeon's reaction to her engagement. She found herself feeling defensive. "Don't you think that since it has been over 4 years since Bomar and I broke up that it's time for me to find genuine happiness with someone else, Napoleon? I do not feel that I can continue being alone like you."

As soon as Goldie had made the last statement, she wanted to take it back. She felt like it was childish and immature of her to say it in view of how Napoleon had only tried to look after her. He was so sincere, honest and caring. But she was a woman and she was not as emotionally strong as he was. Randall had filled a void in her life that she felt kept her wanting to enjoy life. And she did love him. Perhaps not with the intensity that she had felt with Bomar. But Bomar was her first love. She did not expect to recapture that same type of love again. She was moving on. Surely, Napoleon wanted her to be happy. He had become her best friend and confidant over the years. Sometimes, she felt he could be a little too fatherly and over protective.

"Whatever you say, Precious. Just know that you owe it to Randall to be honest first to yourself. Come here to me now. I'm going to give you a big hug. If you are definitely commited to going through with this wedding, then I will be there to support you all the way. Now that I think about it, it has been beeen a while since I've been to a wedding. I guess too many couples have concluded just living together does work. At least when they separate, the legal aspect is not as messy. A wedding sounds nice. Have you set a date?"

Goldie decided she was not going to get caught up in Napoleon's insipid inferences about her upcoming marriage to Randall. Randall had always been the perfect gentleman before and after they started dating. He made her laugh and he was so very patient with her. He was smart and very intelligent, but still sensitive and adventurous. She adored the boyish and yet macho quality that he displayed in his appearance and she found him to be very sexually attractive. He was unselfish and generous too. How could she not love a man like that, especially when he loved her?

"Well, I must give you time to let this big step that you have chosen sink in more deeply. Randle is a good choice. He will be good to you. Excuse me for rushing off. I promised the other ladies in my life that I would visit with them and sample a new stew dish they were considering for Thanksgiving. I'll bring some by for you to taste tomorrow since you will not be here for the holiday. I love you my sweet flower." Napoleon then gave Goldie a quick hug and let himself out.

Goldie decided to prepare for bed. She hoped she would sleep as peacefully tonight as she had while lying in Randall's protective arms. But first, she decided to call Uncle Yetis with the news of her engagement. He seemed somewhat surprised; however he told her that he was happy for her and that he wanted to walk her down the aisle. Next, he put Aunt Soya on the phone. She expressed more enthusiasm than Goldie had expected. Goldie concluded that if was a choice between Randall and Bomar, her aunt would pick Randall. Sleep did come soon for her after she lay down. She dreamed most of the night of floating aimlessly in the sky like a flower looking for a place to land. The flower would fly high up toward the stars and then suddenly fall backwards toward the earth. She could see a pair of arms reaching for the flower. However, the flower would float back up just as the hands seemed to touch it.

Goldie was awaken the next morning by Randall. He wanted to take her to lunch. They were working on a project at different locations. She hoped he could not detect anything different about her demeanor. She believed she was still happy about the engagement. He told her he had called his parents. They were elated.

The trip home for Thanksgiving was pleasant. Randall got a chance to meet Caleb and Greer. They were impressed with him. Caleb however asked her later if she had told him about Bomar. Goldie wondered why Caleb felt that was important. She dismissed any significance to the inquiry and decided he just wanted her to make sure she was making a clean sweep into the relationship. Surely, Caleb didn't think that she was not over Bomar. As for Randall, he really seemed to enjoy his visit. He suggested they return during the summer to really enjoy the beach which he noticed Goldie delighted in as they strolled down one morning and one evening.

After returning home from the Thanksgiving visit, Goldie noticed Randall seemed to be very anxious about them setting a definite wedding date, She decided a June wedding back in Harahan would suit her just fine, especially since Randall seemed to like her hometown. He readily agreed to this. They shared their plans with family and friends. Napoleon said he was looking forward to finally visiting Aunt Soya and Uncle Yetis. He planned to fly down a week before the wedding. Uncle Yetis had insisted that he do this so that the two of them could go fishing.

Toward the end of January, Randall, approached Goldie about eloping. They had spent Christmas with his family. He told Goldie all the planning for the wedding was too over whelming and pompous for him. His parents were planning to hire a tour bus to transport family members who did not want to fly or drive to the wedding. He jokingly told her there was going to be a northern invasion of Harahan by his family. Goldie had to admit that she was actually letting Randall's mother and sisters plan most of the wedding. She wanted them to feel a part of things since the wedding was being held so far away from them. They had been doing a lot of communicating by phone since the announcement of the wedding. Randall's mother had recommended a wedding planner. Goldie had liked the idea. But, Randall's decision to elope was actually welcomed by her. Randall was so pleased that she agreed. They decided to fly to Las Vegas the day before Valentine Day. They felt nobody would be suspicious since the two lovebirds were engaged. They would return two days later.

Goldie had a hard time keeping the elopement a secret from Napoleon and Uncle Yetis. However, she had promised Randall not to tell anyone. The two continued to live apart. Finally, after a month had passed, she informed Randall that she wanted to tell her uncle and Napoleon. Randall agreed and stated he would also inform his parents. They also decided to inform their co-workers who were planning a big wedding shower for them in May. It was now the end of March.

Goldie and Randall's co-workers were very surprised to learn that they had eloped, but they still surprised them with a wedding shower a few weeks later. By this time, they had moved in together. Napoleon was very supportive as he said he would be. Her aunt and uncle were slightly disappointed.

However, Napoleon assured Uncle Yetis that he was still going to make his trip to Harahan without a wedding taking place. On the other hand, Randall's parents were very upset. His mother insisted that the two must fly up to have a small intimate wedding reception with family and a few friends. They were able to get a week off from work. What was to have been a small wedding reception, turned out to be a wedding gala affair. Goldie was sure there were at least 500 hundred people present at the hotel reception ballroom. She and Randall later learned that Mr. Drommaday had paid for the entire event.

Marriage to Randall was wonderful as far as Goldie was concerned. They enjoyed a very close intimacy in and outside of the bedroom. She loved being a wife. Her domestic skills improved. Napoleon visited often. She even had the honor of Mr. Drommaday coming by on a Sunday with Napoleon's mother. She had concluded there was something definitely going on between them. Work still kept her and Randall very busy. They were doing a lot of travelling together. They were beginning to consider buying a home, after 3 years of marriage. Randall was also becoming anxious about starting a family. Goldie felt things were just perfect the way they were. She wanted to wait until they were actually in a new home before having a child. Aunt Soya and Randall's mother were always hinting about a new addition to the family.

Randall decided he would move forward with purchasing home by the fifth year of their marriage. Goldie was initially excited about looking at homes. However, Randall eventually began to realize that something was bothering her. He felt he needed to reassure Goldie that they could afford a home and that he was ready to take on the full responsibility of their financial expenses, since they were also looking at starting a family as well.

"Goldie, I want you to understand that you will not have to return to work if you do not want to after we start our family. Randall hoped this would calm her concerns. He had to admit that sometimes he felt like Goldie was always evasive when he brought up the subject of having a baby. They would both be turning 30 by the end of the year. He felt while it was not urgent that they start a family, he just felt the timing was right. He wanted his children to enjoy the involvement of grandparents in their lives. Also, he wanted to be able to look forward to being at their college graduation and be an involved grandparent as well. "We have always been honest with each other dear. I must tell you that your constant claim that our marriage is going well troubles me sometimes when I bring up the topic of starting a family. I have always shared with you my strong desire to have a family, even if it is only one child."

Goldie finally realized that her constant claim that she was happy with the way things were had caused him to conclude that she had no intentions of having children.

One Saturday morning Goldie woke up to Randall telling her with exasperation, "You are exactly right, Goldie, this marriage is going too well. I am beginning to feel like we are part of some type of perfect little script. You are a good wife, Goldie, but I need more and you are not feeling me. I know you do not want to hurt me. I also know that you do love me in your own special way and will not leave me. This is now the fith year of our marriage. However, I have decided that we are not being honest with each other or ourselves. Therefore, I am letting you know that I am moving out today. I will be staying in a hotel until my job transfer is officially approved by the end of the month. I can no longer compete with Bomar. I am doing this to make things easier for you"

"Bomar! So that is what this is all about, Randall! How did Bomar come between us? I have been faithful to you. I would never jeopardize this marriage to be with Bomar. You are my life! I love you."

Goldie was finding it difficult to fight back the tears. She thought about her phone call to Napoleon a few days ago. She had informed him that after five years of marriage she realized he had been right about her reasons for getting married. However, Napoleon had responding by saying that he had no idea what she was talking about. She could not believe that Napoleon had spoken to Randall. She was overcome with guilt. No, she did not want to hurt this man. She had really tried to let Bomar go although deep down inside, she knew she still cared for him. How could Randall have known? She had not had any contact with Bomar since moving away from Harahan. Her few return trips home did not involve any contact with him. Also, what was this talk about a job transfer? She felt her legs going limp. She managed to walk from the kitchen stove and sat down at the table. She stared blankly at Randall as he sipped on his cup of hot morning tea. He was avoiding eye contact with her.

"You sometimes talk in your sleep, my love." Randall spoke obtrusively. "At first I chose to ignore it. I had learned from your uncle how close you had been to Bomar. He wanted to make sure that I understood what I was competing with. He could tell how much I loved you, but he was concerned about us getting off to a good start.

You have a lot of people who obviously care about you very much. It has only been just recently that you have uttered Bomar's name in your sleep. I even discussed this matter with Napoleon. He informed me that it was a very private and delicate matter that he could not advise me. He did suggest that I talk to you if really bothered me. It has taken me this length f time to get up the courage to talk to you about it, Goldie. But in the meanwhile, I have been doing a lot of thinking about us. I have decided to make things as easy as possible for you. Yes I still love you, girl and I will probably always. If there is another woman in my life, she will have a lot to compete with, the same way as I am competing with Bomar. As for my transfer, it was approved by Mr. Drommaday over a month ago. I will be moving to France to work on several special projects. Mr Drommaday is aware of why I want to make the move."

Goldie was thinking about all of this as she was returning to work after visiting her uncle about three weeks prior to his death. It had been almost a year since her divorce from Randall. They had parted on good terms. He had left everything to her since he was moving out of the states. Napoleon had been simply wonderful in keeping her busy. The replacement for Randall had not been found. She was glad. Chloe and Cade avoided mentioning Randall's name as much as possible. Mr. Drommaday kept them busy and they continued to do good work to his satisfaction. Now she was preoccupied with her uncle's failing health. She was aware that her aunt was having a difficult time, but she never slowed down with her chores and other interest. Uncle Yetis encouraged her to keep up her normal routine as much as possible. He insisted that she not spend the night with him at the hospital.

Goldie always felt that there was something extra special about her Uncle Yetis. Nevertheless, she sometimes suspected that there was something hidden behind the lively spirit that he was always displaying.

As a very young child, she could recall how he would sometimes just sit alone and quietly on the porch at night staring out into the darkness. She would watch him quietly from the living room window and wonder what he was thinking. She never disturbed him. On one occasion, she had gotten up the courage to ask him was he waiting for someone after he came back into the house. His inscrutable response was, "Everybody is waiting on somebody or something, my little one."

Another thing that Goldie found interesting about her Uncle Yetis was the fact that he never saw himself as a victim or tragic figure. He simply saw life as being a series of causes and effects. He told her he caused things to happen and now he was dealing with the effects, one of his favorite quotes was, "For every lie that is told and for every secret that is kept, the truth will unfold stronger than ever." He loved to take Goldie for walks through the small town of Harahan. He would often tell her that she needed to be prepared to look beyond the peaceful surface of the small town atmosphere. Many lives were intertwined in a way that she could never imagine. While in the hospital, he informed her that she should not be surprised to hear more talk about him after his death than when he was alive. Goldie had wanted to ask so many questions, but decided that would be too risky due to his precarious health. She was glad he got his wish to go home. He died at home three weeks after leaving the hospital. She was in shock over his death, although she knew he had tried to prepare her for it.

"Marigold! Marigold!" Two voices in unison were calling her name. Goldie suddenly directed her focus again toward the people at the grave site. She felt it was strange that she immediately recognized both distinct voices and the women those voices belonged to despite the passing of almost 15 years. Most definitely those voices belonged to her two high school friends, Jade and Nadine. Gold was surprised that they took the time to attend the grave side ceremony.

"We knew you would come." said Jade. She was always the more outspoken of the two.

"Just look at them." Marigold thought. "They are greeting me like old times." What a true friend she had turned out to be. She never visited or called anyone the few times she returned to Harahan for brief visits with her Uncle Yetis and Aunt Soya. She realized now that she just moved away and tried to sever her ties. Aunt Soya often told her that she acted as though she had no roots. She ran with the crowd, but she was always the joker in the pack. Nevertheless, Harahan was her home. It did not matter if she acknowledged it. Refocusing on Jade and Nadine, Marigold realized that they were waiting on a cue from her. She held out her arms to hug them. They both rushed toward her.

Jade expressed condolences and stated she was speaking for all the classmates who still lived in Harahan. Marigold found herself a bit overwhelmed by this expression of concern by the old gang that she used to hang out with in view of her lack of on going contact with any of them. She realized it was about how everybody loved Uncle Yetis. He was well known and liked by everyone. As her two classmates looked intently at her, she began to feel like a lifeless mannequin in a department store front display window. It was as though they were scrutinizing her from head to toe. Suddenly, Nadine spoke for the first time. She informed Marigold that she and Jade had decided to come to the gravesite after the funeral despite the downpour. They were hoping to catch up with her there. She noted that she and Jade had been appointed as spokespersons to invite her to come to a soiree' for their senior class at the Waterfront Diner. She would contact her in a few days with more details. Caleb had informed them that she would probably be in town for several weeks. She apologized for mentioning the matter under the circumstances.

Of course, this was totally unexpected for Marigold. She found herself nodding in affirmative and the two ladies seemed very relieved and pleased.

"We had better leave you alone to spend time with your Aunt Soya, "Jade spoke quite hurriedly. "Again, please accept our heartfelt condolences at the lost of Uncle Yetis. He will be dearly missed. He helped me deal with the lost of both of my parents."

The two hugged Goldie again and scurried on their way content with having accompanied their mission. Goldie watched them with mixed emotions. "How pleasingly plump," she thought they had becomed. She also mused, "The two reminded her of two balloons tied securely with strings to a fence. Bouncing and fluttering, fluttering and bouncing, while never really going anywhere."

Marigold continued walking the brief distance to the gravesite. She failed to notice that Aunt Soya was watching her somber approach. The old lady had seen her niece exit the cab. Despite her grief, she was still placid and she gave her neice a sagacious stare when they made eye contact.

"Marigold!" she called through tightly clenched pearly white dentures. "Is your life really that busy?"

Goldie was suddenly too overcome with emotion to try and explain to Aunt Soya about the flight cancellation due to severe thunderstorms. This caused a five hour delay. She also, had taken an economy flight with one layover. As a result she missed her connecting flight. She had not called because she felt the family would have complained that she should have planned to arrive a few days before the funeral instead of the early morning hours of the funeral day. Her uncle's failing health was proving to be more difficult for her to handle than she wanted to admit. Her focus at work was difficult, but she felt she had to keep her mind preoccupied. Her team members were sympathetic and covered for her as much as possible. Mr. Drommaday had reduced their project loads. She felt that the only person that could understand what she was going through was her uncle. Now, she understood what he meant when he told her during her last visit to visit him that funerals were for the living, not the dead. Somehow she managed to muffle an, "I am so sorry, Aunt Soya."

"Hush up child!" was her aunt's abrupt response. "You are not the one with your man buried six feet in a dirt hole in this muddy ground Besides, I've done enough mourning for the both of us these last few days. I do not need you to remind me about my lost. Now, come here and give me a big hug."

The two women embraced. Both were very much aware of each other's pain and despair. Aunt Soya pulled away first holding her niece at arms length. She found herself inspecting her brother's progeny with genuine concern. Finally, she commented, "Child, you're still skin and bones. I can see you're alone. Are you and that husband of yours still separated?"

The younger woman hesitated before responding. Sometimes her aunt had a way of exasperating her with her lack of prudence about discussing matters at appropiate times. She wondered how she was going to be able to deal with her Aunt Soya without Uncle Yetis.

Not the least bit perturbed by Marigold's silence, Aunt Soya questioned her again. "So you have decided to separate from Raymond for good?" she questioned her niece stoicly.

"You know the word is divorced, Aunt Soya. And his name was Randall not Raymond."

"Randall. Raymond. What difference does it make, Marigold? You did not keep him long enough for me to get to know him very well. Baby girl, I mourn for your lost even more than my own. At least, I do have some good memories and children to comfort me."

"Aunt Soya, I can only deal with pain from one source at a time." Goldie responded curtly.

"Pain, my dear child, never comes from one source. I can honestly tell you with all certainty that pain is always an accumalation just like illness." Yetis knew that too. I do not know why he left me here to go on without him. You got to get control of your life, my child."

Goldie was so glad that her aunt could not read her thoughts, although as a child she sometimes wondered about that. She wanted so much to comfort her aunt, but she was feeling so much inner conflict. She had to agree with her aunt that sometimes since her uncle had passed she felt he had been selfish in leaving them to cope with his lost.

"Now, you must listen to me, Marigold. I do not want you to hurry back home. I have already spoken with that always wonderful Mr.

Napoleon. He said the way has been cleared for you to take as long as you need to deal with my Yetis' death. I see you arrived in a cab. Where's your luggage? Quincy is waiting for me in the limousine. Caleb and Greer were given a ride back to the house with some family members they wanted to get there ahead of everyone. The repast is at the house. You can ride back with me. You missed a lot of friends and family at the funeral."

Marigold could tell her aunt was rambling. She wanted to comfort her. She found herself repeating that she was sorry.

"Sorry about what, Marigold? Sorry that you are stuck here with me? Without Yetis, I guess you and I will have to finally get it together."

Goldie ignored those last comments made by her aunt. She gladly accepted the offer of a ride in the limosine. There was no pancea to deal with death she concluded. She and her aunt would have to work through this. She found herself momentarily feeling that Uncle Yetis was actually smiling at them. She then immediately dismissed the feeling. She looked up at the sky and felt comforted by sun beginning to shine brightly.

Inside the funeral car, both women were silent for the entire forty-five minute ride to the house. Quincy would look at them from time to time in his rear view mirror. He thought about how close they were sitting together, but never had two people been more apart.

Goldie found herself reminiscing about the past as the funeral car passed so many familiar sights. She thought about the fact that her parents, Drake and Gwenetta, had left her behind to live with Aunt Soya and her family when she was just six years old. Aunt Soya would often say to her, "Your parents' crazy life style simply did not afford them an opportunity to bring you up properly." Her father was a bartender and her mother was an undiscovered night club singer.

When she lived with her parents in Chicago, Ms Carnegie Bland lived across the hall in their highrise. Ms. Bland took a fancy to her.

Goldie shuddered at the thought of what her life would have been like the first six years were it not for Ms. Bland. Her parents were day sleepers. They took advantage of Ms. Bland's attachment to her. She often found herself staying all day and all night with Ms. Bland. Ms. Bland often told her that if she had not become so attached to Goldie, she would have to call the "Authorities" on her parents. Of course, as a child she never understood who the "Authorities" were and she did not dare ask. She was just glad that Ms. Bland adored her.

As a retired high school English teacher, Ms. Bland was as her parents often said, "a cultured and elegant lady". They told her to always mind Ms. Bland and show her love and respect. Goldie found that very easy to do. Ms. Bland taught her how to read and she read so many wonderful stories to her. She was a very active woman. She attended many social functions. She loved the opera, symphonies, ballets, plays, and art exhibits. She often took her along with her, referring to her as her very agreeable little companion. It was Ms. Bland who introduced her to Beethoven and Mozart. She made a point of letting her friends know that she would be accompanied by her little companion to their monthly bridge club meetings. Ms. Bland found her to be like a sponge. She was such a fast learner and that delighted Ms. Bland very much.

Every Sunday she and Ms. Bland went to 11 a.m. church services. Ms. Bland only went to church once a week. She informed Goldie that she could not afford to put money in more than one collection plate. She also did not believe in tithing, but she contributed generously when the collection plate was passed around. She loved to read out loud from the Bible, especially from the books of Psalms, Proverbs, and Ecclesiastics. As a matter of fact, she was reading to Goldie from her big oversized family Bible when she passed from this life. Goldie was sitting in her favorite little rocking chair positioned in front of her. She was holding her baby doll, "Can Can", who she named after the country of Canada. Suddenly, Ms. Bland started coughing and then her hands loosen their grip on the large Black Bible which fell to the floor with a loud thump. Despite her young age, Goldie knew something was wrong. She ran across the hall to get Drake and Gwenetta. Fortunately, for her it was 7 p.m. and the two of them were awake and sober. They rushed to Ms. Bland's apartment as Goldie screamed something was wrong. Gwenetta entered the apartment first and gasped for breathe as she saw Ms. Bland slumped on the floor. Drake grabbed Gwenetta as though holding her back. Then he let her go and knelt down and felt for Ms. Bland's pulse. He screamed for Gwenetta to call for an ambulance. However, Gwenetta was screaming hysterically. He got up and made the call himself. Then he tried to comfort Gwenetta. Goldie was unable to realize how the impact of what was happening was going to shape her future. At that moment, she just wanted Ms. Bland to sit back up and continue to read out of the Bible. Suddenly, her parents turned their attention to her. Gwenetta had calmed down, but she was still crying, but more sofly. Drake held out his arms to embrace her. She was undecided whether to run to him or away from him. As far as she could tell, the situation was not looking too good for her. She could not understand why Ms. Bland did not get up. How could she leave her alone with Drake and Gwenetta and their crazy life style? This was their night to bake brownies. "Dear God." she thought, "What was going to happen to her." She concluded the "Authorities" would be coming to get her after all. She felt herself fainting as Drake grabbed her.

The week went by very fast. Ms. Bland died on a Sunday. She was buried on a Friday. The funeral was at 12 noon at the church. Goldie wondered if Ms. Bland knew she was going to church on a Friday and at a different time. The funeral was well attended. Goldie found herself being hugged and kissed by so many people. Gwenetta had agreed to let her bring "CanCan". Ms. Bland had bought her the doll after the two of them had gone on a four day trip to Niagara Falls last year. The funeral services were a blur to her. She felt herself unable to focus on what was being said. She tried closing her eyes and imagining that Ms. Bland was sitting next to her. She wondered what Ms. Bland would say about the fact that there was no passing of the collection plate.

A few days after the funeral, Drake told her they were going on a trip to visit his sister. Goldie had noticed that Gwenetta had been doing a lot of packing before the funeral. She figured they would be gone for a while. The idea that her father had a sister was fascinating to her. She had never thought of her parents as being related to anybody.

The ride to Harahan seemed endless to Goldie. Her parents remained relatively quiet during most of the trip. She felt so lonely in the back seat. She snuggled "CanCan" closer to her body. She decided to pretend that Ms. Bland was sitting by the right passenger window side and pointing out interesting sights along the way. After all, Ms. Bland always encouraged her to be very observant. The highway ran along side a considerable stretch of ocean front. Mountains were on the left side as Drake drove headed south. They had left in the wee hours of the morning. Now the sun was rising. She could see the waves softly hitting the rocky shores and then seemingly being tossed back into the ocean's mysterious waters. It was calming for her. Gwenetta handed her a peanut butter and jelly sandwich. She finished it and soon fell asleep.

Goldie was awaken by the sound of Drake honking the car's horn. He was slowly turning into a long winding driveway in a manner that showed he was quite familiar with it. Goldie assumed it was before her time. The driveway ended fewer than three large magnolia trees to the right side of the house. Goldie stared at the house. It reminded her of some homes in the stories that Ms. Bland had read to her. It was a two story white wood framed house with a porch that extended the full length of the front of the house. The screen door and entrance door were painted red. The trimmings around all the windows were also painted red. There was a wooden black swing on the left side of the porch. There were two brown wooden rocking chairs on the right side of the front door. A boy's bicycle was leaning against the front porch near the steps. There were colourful pansies and mums planted around the front of the house. Goldie decided that Ms. Bland would approve of this house. If only, Ms Bland would come out of the front door.

But of course, no Ms. Bland came out of the front door. Instead, a rather portly and petite woman with a colorful bandana around her head appeared. She had on a red apron and she was screaming almost as loud as Drake's car horn sounded. She was upon them so fast. It was as though the house blew her outside. She was screaming for Drake to stop blowing his horn and as Drake got out of the car, she was hugging and clinging to him as though for her dear life.

Almost instantaneously, she was shouting for the other occupants of the house to come outside. As fast as she had grabbed Drake, she grabbed Gwenetta with as much strong emotion. Goldie was somewhat mesmerized by this entire scene and she found herself wanting to get in with the hugging and screaming. When the lady with the bandana reached for her, she ran willingly into her arms. Goldie felt that she smelled refreshingly clean and nice like vanilla and baby oil scent. By this time, the other occupants of the house were outside and the hugging and greeting continued. Goldie had never seen her parents so interactive and expressing so much joy and laughter. It was as though the plump woman with the bandana and apron had pushed a button that activated Drake and Gwenetta. That was Goldie's first encounter with her Aunt Soya who in turned introduced her to Uncle Yetis and her cousins, Caleb and Greer. Unfortunately, Aunt Soya was Drakes only sibling.

The cousins managed to pull Goldie away from the adults as they continued to laugh and talk, and hug and pat on each other as though they were still in awe at seeing each other for the first time in six years. Her cousins quickly informed her that they wanted to show her the bedroom that was to be hers. "A room, you mean my own bedroom?" Goldie questioned. "I am going to have my own room and sleep on a real bed." She could hardly believe that. finally she would have a private bedroom with doors to close and windows to look out of. Even when she stayed with Ms. Bland, she slept on a foldout couch bed the same as at her parents. She was wondering how long would they be with this seemingly nice family. Drake and Gwenetta had not told her anything and she did not know what to expect.

Goldie never questioned her parents about anything. She had already decided that she liked her two cousins. She did not want to ask Drake and Gwenetta anything that might upset them. It had been a long, quiet and somewhat lonely drive for her to arrive at this place. Now, she was feeling excited about everything. She hoped that when she fell asleep tonight she would still wake up in Harahan. Her cousins had told her the name of the small town. They had also promised to take her to the beachfront the next day. In her mind, she could still see the trickling of the waves in the waters and she wanted to see the beach during the day and later at sunset.

Goldie did not have to wait long for the answers to her questions. After breakfast the next morning, she was sitting on the porch swing between Caleb and Greer when Drake and Gwenetta came out of the front door with suitcases. It was around 10 a.m. Goldie felt herself feeling anxious. How could they leave so soon? She avoided eye contact with both of them. Gwenetta kept walking strait toward their parked car. Drake sat the luggage down that he held in both of his hands. He walked toward the swing, half smiling at Goldie. He patted both boys on their heads and then informed them that he needed a moment to speak alone with Goldie. Goldie felt an awkwardness coming over. She did not want the boys to leave her there with Drake. She contemplated getting up and running back into the house. However, she remembered that Ms. Bland was always telling her that her parents really did love her in their own peculiar way. She managed to raise her head without looking directly at her father. Drake sat quietly next to her and then gave her a strong hug. That's when Goldie found herself looking at the two suitcases, neither was the one that Gwenetta had packed her clothing in for the trip. Still, she would not look directly at her father. She focused on the bright living room curtains with their beautiful white lace trimmings. She liked this house with its large rooms, high ceilings and hardwood floors. The house was warm and inviting. It had lots of windows. She loved the openness of this house. Her parents seldom opened the curtains in their apartment. Even though, she liked Ms. Bland's apartment, she still felt that it was rather small, but cozy.

Drake gradualy released his hold on her. He cleared his throat as though preparing to say something when suddenly the honking of the car horn, obviously by Gwenetta, interrupted him. Drake stood up and asked her to walk with him to the car. Next, he informed Goldie as they walked slowly that he and Gwenetta were leaving her with Aunt Soya and her family for a while. He said that he and Gwenetta would probably return to pick her up in about six or seven months. He felt that she would enjoy her stay with Aunt Soya and she was delighted to have her. He said that living with his sister would be more stable for her until he and Gwenetta got settled. Gwenetta was hoping to get her singing career off the ground again and he was her temporary manager. They had some promising offers in Los Angeles, California and Las Vegas which was going to be their first stop.

Goldie had listened with mixed emotions as Drake shared this information with her. Of course, at the time she did not fully comprehend what Drake was saying. But, she felt that leaving her behind to live with Aunt Soya, Uncle Yetis, and the boys was not a bad idea. She did not want Drake to realize that she was pleased with their decision to leave her behind. She did realize that it would be an adjustment for her. She was use to seeing her parents every day although she spent a lot of time with Ms. Bland. Were they going to leave her like Ms. Bland? She decided she had to go along with the decision to leave her behind. There were so many things about her parents that she wanted to know and she felt like living with her Aunt Soya would provide her with some answers. She also believed as Ms Bland would have said, "They were good people who loved her in their own peculiar way."

"You have always been a big girl about handling things. I feel you have a maturity well beyond your age little girl." Drake appeared to sound a little proud of her, Goldie thought. "I can tell you like it here already." Drake interjected. "Gwenetta and I have big plans for your future. We will be staying in touch while we are gone. I love you girl." The last statement by Drake caught Goldie by surprise. She did not ever recall hearing him or Gwenetta say those words to her. It filled her with a bitter/sweetness.

As they finally approached the car, Goldie was suddenly aware that everybody was gathered there.

Caleb and Greer had run ahead with Drake's suitcases. Gwenetta got out of the car as she and Drake got closer. She let go of Drake's hand and ran to give Gwenetta a hug. She actually felt Gwenetta hugging her back much to her delight. She also found it amusing when Gwenetta informed her to be good and help Aunt Soya around the house with the cooking and cleaning. Her mother hated any type of domestic work around the home. Drake did the majority of the cooking and cleaning when it was done. There were many occassions when she and Ms. Bland would clean up because Ms. Bland said it would keep the "Authorities" away.

Goldie had been six years old when her parents turned around and drove back to the main highway. She had watched in silence until the car could no longer be seen. She realized years later that her parents' life had gotten back on track that day the way they had intended before she came along and interrupted their plans. She had been a temporary detour. "They did," as Aunt Soya would say, "try to do right by her." They could not have left Goldie in better hands. Aunt Soya and Uncle Yetis took over what Ms. Bland had started in the care of the precious and precocious young lady. Also, she had gained two cousins who were more like older brothers to her. Goldie found Aunt Soya's family to be very intact and fun loving. She often wondered how Aunt Soya and Drake could have been biologically related.

An entire year passed before Goldie heard from Drake. He finally wrote her a letter. Goldie was aware that from time to time that he called Aunt Soya who seemed to become upset when he called. She never informed Goldie about the nature of the calls. Goldie assumed they would eventually show up to get her. She just hoped it would not happen before she graduated from school. She learned to distance herself from her past, choosing only to remember Ms. Bland.

In the beginning, Caleb and Greer kept her preoccupied. Caleb was five years older than her. Greer was ten years older. They both adored her and were amazed over her academic skills. She also was very flexible and had a somewhat tomboyish side to her that made it easy for them to have her tag along on their many adventuresome escapades. They spent many summer days exploring up and down the beachfront strip, discovering caves, fising, swimming, and enjoying late evening cookouts with friends. Goldie fell in love with the sandy shores. She loved the evening hours as the sun set. Often the three of them would look out at the horizon and talk about their dreams for the future. In time, Goldie began to feel an inner calm that she had not experienced since Ms. Bland's death.

Aunt Soya was right, Goldie thought. Pain never comes from one source. It was always an accumulation. She found herself snuggling closer to her aunt in the limousine. She longed to be that happy little girl running and laughing along the beech front with her cousins at sunset.

Aunt Soya remained silent, but she was comforted by her niece moving closer to her. They had been so close at one time. She had only wanted to make life better for her children. At the same time, she wanted them to be strong, independent, caring and intelligent. The world was changing so fast as they were growing. As their world expanded, she often felt like she and Yetis could no longer protect them. Now, she was having a hard time accepting Yetis' death. How could she comfort her family if she did not feel comforted? She kept thinking about the minister's comments that her Yetis had been called to be with the Lord. She had to admit that she did not find anything comforting about her Yetis being with the Lord in heaven. She could not imagine Yetis being in the company of the Lord anywhere. The old coon had drunk himself to death. And as far as she knew, there were no drunks in heaven. She had been with Yetis since she was nineteen years old. Fifty-three years of loving him would not be easily forgotten. The pain in her heart was deep and she felt that coping with death was taking a toll on her faith.

Aunt Soya recalled Yetis had started drinking shortly after Caleb was born. Prior to that, his major vice had been gambling. Eventually, he completely stopped gambling, but she was never able to compete with the booze. It did not appear that her love was strong enough to comfort him anymore. She knew that he still loved her, but his drinking binges became too frequent. It was as though he was dealing with a nightmare that haunted him. He would tell her that everything was alright and that he was not going to drink himself to death. She would tell him that she felt he was determined to die ahead of her so that he would not have to deal with the pain of her loss. He would just laugh at her and tell her that that was the craziest thing that he ever heard.

Goldie sensed her aunt's pain. She remembered how she thought that her aunt was certainly no Ms. Bland. As a matter of fact, the only thing that the two had in common was their love for her. Aunt Soya was always going to church on Sundays and during the week. She served on several committees and song in the choir. She was unable to infuse this spiritual thirst in the other household members. Uncle Yetis and the boys were sporadic in their attendance. Goldie managed to convince her aunt to continue allowing her to attend 11 a.m. services. Her aunt only had a 9th grade education, but she was a very bright and intelligent woman. She was an excellent seamstress and wonderful cook. She had a small vegetable garden and did canning during the summer. She loved books and believed in having an in home library. When she realized how well her niece could read, she would often have Goldie read to her when she was cooking in the kitchen or sewing. She was also very outspoken. Goldie loved her strong sense of family. Her aunt was somewhat fussy, but she had a sense of humour and it was obvious that Uncle Yetis and the boys loved her dearly. Goldie grew to feel the same way.

Goldie also thought that her aunt was a very attractive woman. She tended to downplay her good looks because her dress was simple. She dressed more for comfort than style. She always seemed to have an apron tied around her wasteline. She was a full figured woman with nice legs that she tended to cover up with dresses or skirt lengths below the knees. Her face was round with well defined cheek bones that gave her a very youthful appearance. She always appeared to have a smile on her face. Her hair was long, but she wore it combed back in a bond and a slight part in the middle. She would wear it down on special occassions and some Sundays. She did not wear glasses. Goldie often marvelled at how her aunt seemed oblivious to the many admiring looks that she got from men whenever they were out in public.

Her aunt was also very protective of her sons and Goldie. Goldie thought about the time her aunt defended her when she first started school in Harahan. Drake and Gwenetta had failed to enroll her in school, so there were no school records to assist in determining her academic level and her social skills with children her age were almost non-existent. She preferred hanging out with older kids. Fortunately, Ms. Bland had done a good job of teaching her how to read and write.

She also possessed good math and geography skills. She was placed in first grade, but her teacher soon realized she was too advanced and then there was the problem with interacting with the other students in her class whom Goldie felt were immature and not very bright. Aunt Soya had tried to warn the school about her very intelligent niece. Nevertheless, Aunt Soya felt that Goldie had been robbed of her childhood and she wanted her to have more interaction with children her age. The school finally agreed to put her in split classes. She was placed in a third grade class for all of her academic subjects except for art, music and physical education. The teachers were very impressed with Goldie, but she had very few friends. Some parents protestested that she was being shown favoritism. Goldie became the talk of the town. Eventually, some parents insisted on having a meeting with Aunt Soya, and the school principal. Aunt Soya was agreeable to this without realizing that their mission was to suggest that Goldie be home schooled. The meeting was held at her aunt's home on a Friday evening. She was not allowed to be present. However, the meeting shortly took a turn for the worse when the idea of home schooling Goldie was suggested. The general consensus was that "Goldie was too smart for her own good and she was too much of a distraction for the other students."

Goldie insisted on wearing only dresses to school. She also did not wear tennis shoes to school. She always wore bangs and her hair was always in a ponytail. She did not like braids or plaits. Ms Bland deserved credit for her dress preference and hair style. Some of the parents felt she was too snobbish and critical of her peers. This time, Aunt Soya felt the school and the parents had over reacted. She politely asked them to leave her home and informed them that as far as she was concerned her niece was probably the most normal child at the school. She even believed that one day Goldie would become the first female principal at the school and they needed to try and live with that thought. After this situation occurred, Uncle Yetis worried that they might be shunned by the entire town. Harahan only had one elementary school and one high school. However, Aunt Soya and Goldie had a good laugh about the entire matter. There was no other school for Goldie to attend and her aunt and uncle were in no position to home school Goldie. Her aunt also knew the school had no right to refuse to allow Goldie to continue as a student. Nevertheless, they both looked forward to summer vacations.

By the second year, Goldie's school life was beginning to quiet down. She still did not have any close friends beside Dakota Winston, who lived behind her aunt's home. They were the same age and were total opposites in terms of their personalities. Uncle Yetis said they complimented each other. Her aunt was not extremely fond of Dakota, but she was glad that Goldie had one female friend. Things did eventually change at school when Goldie scored in the 100 percentile on all of her achievement test scores. She out performed every student in the elementary school district. A newspaper article was written about her test scores and the local television stations aired this acheivement as well. Her aunt and uncle were so proud of her. Her popularity at school improved. Goldie was taken aback by all of the attention. She could not understand all of the fuss over something that came so natural for her. However, she and Aunt Soya were relieved that she was finally being viewed in a more positive way.

Goldie's outstanding academic performance continued throughout her school years. She was able to complete high school at the age of sixteen. She was also given special allowance to attend a nearby state university.

Goldie reflected on how her life had been rather uneventful, despite her initial integration into the public school system. in Harahan College seemed to be following the same course until fate allowed her path to cross with Bomar's. She starting smiling as she recalled her aunt referring to him as the "Plague". Bomar had entered her life when she was eighteen and her life was never the same. She had dated ocassionaly while in high school because her aunt insisted that she should. However, she was never seriously interested in anyone. She was surprised when she found an instant attraction to Bomar. It was more than she bargained for and she found that her first encounter with cupid's arrow was deep and binding. She was most definitely in love and there was nothing Aunt Soya could do to change matters. It was time for her aunt to stop thinking of her as her little baby girl. That was the beginning of her pulling away from Aunt Soya.

Quincy was already slowing down in front of the house before his two passengers realized it. A few cars were parked on the grassy yard. It was obvious that there was a lot of activity going on in and outside of the house. The sun was beginning to set. Quincy got out of the limousine and opened the door for his passengers. Goldie was thanking him when she suddenly found herself being grabbed from behind and lifted into the air. "Goldie! Goldie! My dear little Baby Girl! I knew you were coming!" screamed the deep masculine baritone voice of the party that was handling her like she was an over-sized ragged doll. That voice could only belong to her cousin, Greer. He was an impressive 6' 5" tall over grown boy as far as she was concerned. She was not sure how Aunt Soya was feeling about this outward display of affection. She decided not to look in her direction. When Greer finally put her down, she hugged him and whispered in his left ear that this behaviour was not to be repeated. They both laughed. It made Goldie feel better. Before she could ask him, he informed her that Caleb was in the house. Then he mockingly informed her that all of her worldly possessions were in her bedroom. A nice taxi driver had dropped them off and she owed him for paying the taxi driver. Then he winked at her. Goldie realized Greer was trying to keep her in a good mood. She could see the hurt in his eyes and she was sure that he could see her pain. He had been so close to his father.

Greer escorted her to the front steps. "Caleb is looking forward to seeing you." he informed her. "Do not look so sad, Baby Girl. We will pull through this. Now let me get back to mother. She's watching us and I know that you need a break from her after that ride from the gravesite. I love you." Greer kissed her on the forhead and was off to attend to his mother who was still standing near the limosine. She was surrounded by friends and family. He could discern that she was tired and needed to be rescued.

Goldie found herself being grabbed and hugged and kissed by many of the household occupants as she tried to locate Caleb. Finally, she heard his voice coming from the kitchen. She should have known to look there first. Aunt Soya's kitchen had always been the family's place to gather. Some homes had dens, but for them the largest room in the house was the kitchen and it was very spacious. Her uncle and aunt were good cooks. She had so many fond memories of tasty dishes and enticing food odors. Many lively discussions were also held around the kitchen table.

Caleb was sitting in his favorite spot at the kitchen table. Another slightly older man was seating across from him. They were the only ones seated. Caleb introduced him as Jackson Adair, a long time friend of Greer who had moved to Harahan about nine months ago from Orlando, Florida. He stood up and gave Goldie a hug and expressed his personal condolences regarding Uncle Yetis death. He also pulled out a chair for Goldie to sit in and then excused himself. He was going to see if he could locate Aunt Soya or Greer. Caleb remained seated and appeared relaxed. He was drinking a beer. The table held many appetizing dishes. The other occupants in the kitchen were busy trying to prepare plates and keep others from loitering in the kitchen. It did appear to be somewhat chaotic. Goldie did not recognize the four ladies who were trying to keep an eye on things. She did notice one in particular giving Caleb a lot of attention. She had to admit that her cousin had grown to become a very handsome man. It always amazed her that Caleb was so much like his father, but he was Aunt Soya's favorite. He and Uncle Yetis had many confrontations during his youthful years. Drinking had also become one of his pass times. Aunt Soya had insisted as the children were growing up that no liquor be brought into the house. It was a mystery to her how Caleb became so attached to drinking, when Greer completely stayed away from any kind of alcoholic beverage.

Caleb looked up and nodded as Goldie sat down at the table. "Little G," he said. "You are still looking good girl and that is not my liquor that's talking. Excuse me for not getting up, but these ladies have stuffed me and now I'm waiting for one of them to throw me in that oven."

"You seem to have taken good care of yourself, Caleb. I'm sorry about missing the funeral."

"Well, you know how I hate funerals. I could tell you were there in spirit. I appreciated the beautiful live mums and pansies that you sent Poppa. You were the only person that remembered those were poppa's favorite flowers. Baby girl, you sent so many I was beginning to wonder if there was a second funeral."

"Well, I'm relieved to know that the flowers arrived on time even if I didn't, Caleb. How did Aunt Soya manage during the services?"

"You know mom, Little G, always the pillar of strength in public. Greer and I have been trying to hang around, but out of her way at the same time. I'll be here for another 10 days before flying back to Atlanta. You know, I didn't realize how much I missed this place. Sitting here in the kitchen brings back a lot of memories. I loved that old man. I put him through a lot of changes, but he was always there for me."

"I know how you feel, Caleb. I'm beginning to feel the same way. We had a good life. Aunt Soya and Uncle Yetis gave us their heart and soul. Who could ask for more?"

Sitting down at the table, Goldie found herself looking out the back kitchen window. She could still see a full view of Ms. Beulah Mae's house. "How is Ms. Beulah Mae doing?" Goldie asked her cousin in an attempt to change the subject. She was trying to keep her composure. She felt that Caleb was having a difficult time as well.

"She is holding on. She does not get out much these days. She did not make it to the funeral, but Dakota did and in grand style as usual. I'll let momma tell you about that. As far as I'm concered, Dakota was probably the only live person at the funeral."

Goldie noticed a smile surfaced as Caleb made reference to Dakota. Dakota was Ms. Beulah Mae's niece. She and Dakota had developed a very close bond growing up in Harahan. She wondered what had Dakota been up to since she moved away. Dakota had been her best friend, but she was very upset when Goldie informed her that she was accepting the job offer out of town. She refused to accompany Stephano to the airport to see her off and she failed to attend the going away dinner that Aunt Soya invited her to the day before Goldie left town. Goldie refused to call her whenever she returned to visit her aunt and uncle. They were both very stubborn. Uncle Yetis had often insisted that she needed to put forth more effort in reaching out to Dakota. "She needs you more than you need her, Goldie. Don't totally abandon her." Uncle Yetis would inform her time and time again.

"I feel a need to get away from this crowd, Caleb. I'm going to walk across the bottom to see Ms. Beulah Mae."

"That's a good thought, Baby Girl. I'm sure she's probably sitting on the porch listening to all the activity going on around here. Tell her hello for me. I'll try to make a special visit to see her before I leave."

Goldie could see that Ms. Beulah Mae was awake since lights appeared to be on in several rooms of the red brick house. As a child, she had marvelled at the fact that Ms. Beulah Mae's house was brick with a concrete porch. Most of the homes in the neighborhood were wood with wooden porches. Ms. Beulah Mae's husband had been a building contractor. "If you imagine it, it can be built." was his motto. He made sure that his home had all of the modern conveniences. There was an attached two car garage. The house had indoor plumbing and air conditioning long before most of the other homes did in that neighborhood. The yard was beautifully landscaped and there was a small pond on the back side of the house. It was deep enough and clean enough when she was growing up to go swimming in. Her cousins had taught her to swim in it before she started swimming in the ocean. She and Dakota had become friends shortly after she arrived in Harahan. However, Dakota attended a private boarding school and so Goldie only got to see her during the summer months. The two did eventually develop a very close friendship. Aunt Soya was not particulary fond of Dakota, because she felt there was something "strange" about that child. On the other hand, Ms. Beulah Mae adored Goldie. In fact, Goldie and the boys were the only children in the neighborhood that she allowed to visit.

Goldie thought about how she had loved to spend the night with Dakota who started living with Ms. Beulah Mae when she was three years old. Dakota also had an older brother, Delroy. Their mother, December, was Ms. Beulah Mae's older sister. She died from breast cancer. She never married their father. When she learned that she had breast cancer, she asked Ms. Beulah Mae if she and her children could move in indefinitely. The cancer proved to be very aggressive. She died a year later. Ms. Beulah Mae's husband, Cyrus, had insisted that the children remain with them. There had been some talk among family members of separating them. Cyrus had become very attached to the children. He had always wanted children of his own; however after ten years of marriage he had concluded that he and his wife were going to be childless.

"Is that you, Marigold?" A very familiar and very soft voice called out to Goldie from the screened in front porch. Ms. Beulah Mae had the porch screened in when her eyesight started diminishing.

"You have an uncanny sense of knowing who is approaching you, Ms Beulah Mae." Goldie spoke tenderly to her as she opened the screened door to the porch. Upon entering, she gave Ms. Beulah Mae a kiss on the cheek and a pat on her back.

"I knew you would come and see me. You got a lot of Uncle Yetis in you. He was always checking on me after Cyrus died. Even when he was drunk, he would call himself checking on me. You remember how you kids would try to help me sober him up sometimes when he stopped by before going home to Aunt Soya. He really did love that woman. I could see how he suffered immensely from that one act of unfaithfulness."

Goldie found herself at a lost of words when Ms. Beulah Mae made her last statement about her uncle as though it was common knowledge. She recalled growing up that Mr. Beulah Mae seemed to always know a lot about what was going on in the small town of Harahan. She wanted to pursue this revelation in more details, but she decided to address it later. She would discuss this with her cousins. She did however politely tell Ms. Beulah Mae that her uncle had so much going on at times that it was difficult to know what was true or hearsay because of his drinking.

"Whatever you say, child, Life is full of surprises and twists and turns. Now go in the house and fix you a plate. Dakota left about two hours ago. She cooked dinner and said she was taking some food over to your aunt's house. She went to the funeral. She told me you did not make it in time for the funeral, but that you were at the gravesite for the burial. You two need to get together again. Your Uncle Yetis and I often discussed how the two of you were more stubborn than two mules. Friendship is not something you need to let go. It can be more precious than family. Dakato has not been the same since you moved away. That child wore all white to the funeral. She had on a white hat, white dress, white gloves, white shoes and she told me all her foundations were white. She even pinned a white rose to her dress. She informed me when she got back from the funeral that some kid had asked her if she was an angel. We both had a good laugh about that. I didn't make it to the funeral. I want you to know it was not due to my health, but that is what everybody is saying. I was very close to Yetis. He was the only man, besides my Cyrus that I trusted and could talk to. Some times I felt he understood me better than Cyrus. Please give your aunt my personal condolences. I will call her in a day or too. She definitely was very supportive and helpful when Cyrus died. Right now, I must try deal with my own hurt. I still can not believe Yetis is gone. I can not imagine what that must be like for your aunt."

Goldie assured Ms. Beulah Mae that she was going to let Aunt Soya know to expect a call within a few days. Goldie wanted to ask where did Dakota live, but decided she could probably get the information from Greer. He had never moved away from Harahan. He was able to move out on his own when he was nineteen. He had landed a job with the railroad company and much to his parents' disappointment refused to go to college or a trade school. However, he was a sensible young man who wisely spent and saved his money. He was able to buy his own home in his late twenties. He had travelled overseas on several occasions. He showered Aunt Soya with gifts. His father grew to be very proud of him. They did a lot of father and son things together. Greer bought his father his first riding lawn mower and his first motor boat. Goldie had secretly wanted Greer and Dakota to get together, but it never happened. Greer treated her like a little kid sister the same way that he treated Goldie. Several local girls had pursued him, but he never remained in a long term relationship. Goldie was beginning to think there would be no one left to carry on the family's name. Caleb was married twice, but had no children. She was also childless. Perhaps, grandchildren would have been a good distraction for Uncle Yetis.

"Goldie, I was surprised to see Dakota show up and prepare such a wonderful dinner. She told me not to say a word to her. She still has this thing about cleaning. She shows up most mornings and cleans up for me as well as prepares me a hot meal. She usually finishes around noon. I guess you know that she and Emerson Gant are divorced. Emerson has the kids. Dakota had a hard time coping with that. But she has always been there for me. I just leave her alone to do as she pleases. She is still just as pretty now as she was when she was a child. The kids simply adore her. Emerson allows her to visit the children weekly. He will not allow her to have them for an overnight stay. Emerson knows she is a good mother. I think he feels she might try to run off with them. The school allows her to drop in on them sometimes during lunch time. I am sure Emerson knows about that, but he does not try to stop her. I guess you are tired of listening to an old woman ramble on and on. I don't get much company. Your Uncle use to come by often before his health starting failing him. You know he called me the day before he died. Can you believe that he was concerned about how I was doing? We talked for about an hour. His voice sounded strong. He told me he was at peace. He said being thankful and forgiving can carry you a long way. He said next to your aunt's situation, accepting that Greer was gay was a big obstacle for him to overcome. Your aunt refuses to acknowledge it. I hope she can handle it now that Yetis is gone. Greer and his friend come by to see me sometimes. His name is Jackson. I never thought I would ever say it, but I actually look forward to their visits. Jackson is an accountant. He helps me with my bills and other business matters. He also helped me write my will. They are very entertaining. Jackson can play the piano and Greer sings several jazz numbers that I like. I know that you have not met Jackson, but Uncle Yetis wanted me to make sure that you knew about him. Jackson also helped Uncle Yetis write his will. Sometimes Jackson went along on the fishing trips with Greer and your uncle. "

Greer, gay? That was certainly news to Goldie. She had no clue when Caleb introduced Jackson as Greer's long time friend. Why would her aunt and uncle keep so much information from her? She decided not to pursue this sharing of information from her uncle via Ms. Beulah Mae. She and Dakota definitely needed to talk. Her only response to her neighbor was, "I have not had a chance to see Dakota and where is Delroy? Did he make it to the funeral? I forgot to ask my cousins about him."

"Delroy's dead, Marigold." Ms. Beulah stared straight ahead not giving Goldie any eye contact. She shook her head side to side and then lowered it."

Gold was surprised by this revelation from her neighbor. "How could that be, Ms. Beulah Mae? No one has said anything to me. When was the funeral? What happened?"

Goldie was having a difficult time controlling her emotions. Aunt Soya and Uncle Yetis were confronting so many issues; her relationship with Bomar and her decision to move away, Caleb's drinking and now news to her, Greer's gayness. She was sure Uncle Yetis wanted her to know about Greer, but why now? She was also experiencing guilt for not being there for Dakota? Why had no one informed her of Delroy's passing? He had been relatively close to Greer. She was beginning to feel that everyone was keeping too much from her. Should she believe Ms. Beulah Mae? Her aunt had often warned her to weigh carefully what Ms. Beulah said at times. She decided to calm down and ask a few more questions about Delroy.

"What did Delroy die from Ms. Beulah Mae and when was the funeral?" she inquired with more self control.

"The funeral has been going on all his life, Marigold. He died when he closed his eyes to life. Now he is buried in the P.P.C."

Goldie found herself more baffled by this response. Delroy had always been a rather quiet young man. He had piercing black eyes. Goldie thought he was handsome in a peculiar way, but she did not see any resemblance between him and his sister, Dakota. However, the two of them were very close. At times, he could be very protective of Dakota. He was four years older. He developed a friendship with both Caleb and Stephano. Goldie found him to be polite, but she did not feel drawn to him. He had been her escort to one high school dance at the insistence of her aunt who was very impressed with his quiet demeanor. He was a perfect gentleman and he was also a better dancer than Goldie, much to her surprised. His Uncle Cyrus had insisted that he be allowed to attend public schools. Goldie remembered that he was very fond of his uncle.

Goldie could not recall a graveyard in Harahan named P.P.C. There was definitely something inscrutable about this conversation that she was having with Ms. Beulah Mae. She was beginning to conclude that there was something going on behind these brick walls that might explain Dakota's sometime eccentric behavior. She decided she needed to know where P.P.C was located.

"I'm not familiar with a cemetery called P.P.C., Ms. Beulah Mae. Marigold tried to be very placid. She could discern Ms. Beulah Mae was in some kind of deep thought.

"Well, I am glad to know that, Goldie. Delroy, I am afraid has gone AWOL. He's in the People's Prison Camp and now he is absent without life. The last time I saw him, he told me that he was going through joint pains and that he did not need me to come around any more. I told him I was going through joint pains too. He was hooked on dope and now he was locked up in the joint. I was hooked on him and could not bare to see him in the joint. He was trying to let the dope go and I was trying to let him go. Cyrus' death took a toll on that young man. He just tried to just stay in his room all the time and smoke that stuff. I told him that as long as he lived in my house he would have to show me some signs of life. There was plenty to do to keep him busy. My house was no morgue. I did not house dead bodies. He and his sister walked in the front doors and I would see to it that they walked out of the same doors. I love Delroy and Dakota like they were my own children, but they always seemed to gravitate toward

Cyrus even though they were my sister's children. I am still trying to understand where I went wrong. I know that if Cyrus had lived things would have been different. Delroy just got to hanging with the wrong crowd after Cyrus' death. Dakota tried to be strong for both of us. She missed you so much when you moved away. You know, she once told me that she thought about leaving Harahan and surprising you. I know she has stayed in Harahan because of me, her brother and the kids. Life can be very burdensome, Goldie."

Goldie was trying to decide what to say to Ms. Beulah Mae who obviously had a lot on her mind. "Ms Beulah Mae, in life you make choices and you have to live with the consequences of those choices. That is something Uncle Yetis was always telling me. Everything has a price. You can not make credit charges in life and then try to file bankruptcy when the going gets tough. There's always a payment due. For some us the payback may mean our life."

"Yes you are Uncle Yetis' child. That sounds like something he would say. I'm afraid that I am beginning to get tired. Goldie, will you help me into the house? I've been sitting too long and my legs are stiff. You need to be getting back home. I am sure that my niece will make an appearance to see you before the night is gone. That child has really missed you. Oh by the way, I enjoyed your parents' visit shortly before you came. You are all good people."

Goldie responded to her neighbor's request to assist with helping her get back into the house. She also gave her a hug and a kiss after they got back inside the house. "I will stop by to see you before I leave." she informed Ms. Beulah Mae in what she hoped sounded like a gentle and calm voice. The comment about her parents had been disturbing and surprising to her. Aunt Soya had not mentioned anything about her parents being present for the funeral. She wondered if Caleb and Greer knew. Funerals, she thought, were notorious for reuniting families and revealing family secrets she concluded." She was beginning to feel giddy. She knew she needed to eat something. Perhaps, she could better assimilate all the information that Ms. Beulah Mae was sharing with her. She was feeling somewhat discomposed.

Goldie was relieved to see most of the vehicles were gone when she returned to her aunt's house. She hoped this meant that the majority of the guest had left. She was feeling physically tired and emotionally drained. She found herself recalling Uncle Yetis' comment about how did the word funeral get fun in it. A funeral was definitely no 'fun at all'. She was preparing to knock on the back door when a pair of very soft hands covered her eyes. The very pungent scent of magnolia blossoms kept her from screaming for dear life. Only her girlfriend, Dakota, could wear that scent.

"Dakota, don't you ever sneak up on me like that again. Considering my frame of mind, I might have done something that I would later regret. Now give me a big hug before, I decide to show you some of my Kung Fu that I learned in college."

"I still see that you have the gift of a vivid imagination, my friend. I have missed that effervescent smile and lively disposition that you always displayed growing up. You always seemed to be in control until you met Bomar. Your aunt told me you would be here for a few more weeks. There is so much that we need to catch up on. I'm sure that my Aunt Beulah Mae told you a lot without telling you much in her erratic way. Let's sit at the kitchen table and talk a while. I will fix you a plate. You are thinner than me."

"It does appear to be quiet in the kitchen right now, Dakota. I am hungry. Of course, I have no idea where everyone is at this time. I would love to have your company. I want to ask you about Delroy and a few other matters."

"Aunt Beulah told you that he was dead, didn't she?"

Yes she did. But I figured it out. You do not appear to be upset."

"Before you make a federal case about it, I want you to know that my aunt is not very well at this time. Her eyesight is failing her. She also insists on being the deliver of news in this town. She spends most of her days in front of the TV or listening to the radio. She also has several friends who call her everyday and cater to her nosiness. Her eyesight is not getting any better. I am trying to allow her to remain in her home as long as s possible. She has good days and bad days. I am glad she knew who you were as well as your parents. They were her only visitors today. Most people just shy away from her. Now that Uncle Yetis has passed, her only occasional visitors are some of the ladies from the church, Greer and his friend, and Bomar since he moved back to Harahan. He always brings her photos to look at and this seems to help her a lot. You know Bomar still misses you, Goldie. Caleb told me about your marriage situation. I hope you are doing alright, my friend. I hope you don't mind my saying but you should at least talk to Bomar before you leave."

So Dakota knew about Greer which Goldie decided was not surprising. However, she found herself rushing to interrupt her friend. "Let's not bring Bomar into the conversation, Dakota. I was not going to mention anything about Emerson to you tonight."

"What is it you want to know about me and Emerson Gant, Goldie? I can sum it up in three words, Big Fat Mistake! I am not ashamed to admit that, and you can say, "I told you so!" "But if I had it to do all over again, I would not change a single thing. My two beautiful babies mean the world to me."

Suddenly, Dakota let out a groan that made Goldie realize the deep dispair that only a mother could feel for a child. She herself could only reach out and hold Dakota's hands. Not being able to be with her children when ever she wanted to had to be very painful for her. How could Emerson put her through this misery? Perhaps, Napoleon might know a good lawyer that could help. She recalled how she had tried to talk Dakota out of marrying Emerson. It did not make sense for her beautiful woman like Dakota to marry a man because of his money. Emerson Gant had happen into Dakota's life just as unexpectedly as Bomar had entered hers. She was also eighteen when she met the rich, handsome, charming, but very controlling Emerson. He was seven years older than Dakota. Goldie knew that Emerson was fascinated with the youthful, beautiful, and coquettish Dakota. She also realized that he would quickly tire of Dakota as soon as the fascination played out. However, Dakota was determined that she was going to marry a rich man before she turned twenty-one. Goldie had often felt like she and Dakota should have switched their first names.

Dakota was infected with an insatiable desire to marry into a prominent and rich family in Harahan. She had concluded with her good looks her odds were better if she married young. She was also tired of being a nobody in Harahan. She admired Goldie' smartness. She also thought her friend was very pretty. With those two impressive traits, she felt Goldie would marry successfully in due time. However, she lacked Goldie's smartness and decided she had to get away from her aunt as soon as possible. Her uncle had died her senior year in highschool. He drowned during a fishing trip with Delroy and some other friends. Delroy never got over the death of their uncle. Dakota had decided she could not leave Harahan because she felt her aunt and Delroy needed her. But she did not want to continue living in the house with them. She needed her own life. Emerson's attraction to her was exactly what she wanted. If the son of the richest man in town wanted to date her, then she was going to get him to the altar and deal with the love Jones later. She decided pregnancy was the best entrapment. Goldie was in shock when Dakota told her what she was planning. Nevertheless, after nine months of dating, Dakota informed Emerson that she was pregnant. His parents insisted that he do right by Dakota. Dakota found herself walking down the aisle when she was 3 month's pregnant grinning from ear to ear. Goldie found herself participating in this scandalous affair as the maid of honor. Emerson's family did not want "a known nullius filius" in the family. Dakota had refused to take the money that was offered her to quietly leave town. Emerson was told to marry her for the time being. Poor Dakota, she did not realize that all marriages were not until death do you part.

The Gants had no grandchildren in the family. They adored their beautiful granddaughter, Emerald, with unexpected joy. She was first of all beautiful, and she definitely had the look of a "Gant". She would be raised properly. They would give Dakota a year to do her motherly duty. However, things were postponed when Emerson Gant the third was born 12 months later. Something else happened that Dakota had not planned. She actually fell in love with her husband. However, the feeling was not mutual. Emerson was a wonderful father. He gave all of his time and attention to the children. He became increasingly more distant with Dakota. He eventually moved into his own bedroom shortly after Emerson, Jr was born. They had no social life. Dakota was an excellent home maker and an excellent cook. And although she was a wonderful mother as well, he eventually filed for divorce from Dakota after four years of marriage. Dakota had quietly agreed to the divorce. Emerson's alienation of affection took a toll on her. She did not fight over custody of the children. She agreed that their father's family had more to offer them in terms of a secure future. She was also well provided for financially by Emerson. She did not have to work and he bought her a home near her aunt. When Aunt Soya had told her about Dakota's divorce, Goldie had felt that Dakota needed to get her priorities straight.

"I am here now, Dakota. If it's anything that I can do to help you, you must tell me." Goldie was trying to be strong for Dakota. How could she have not realized the impact that the divorce had on her friend?

"Thanks, Baby Girl. I am sorry for wallowing in my own self pity when you've lost your uncle. I am going to be alright. As Aunt Beulah Mae would say, "I go in and out like that sometimes." My children are being well taken care of and I get to see them quite often. Now, let me tell you about that brother of mine. He is certainly not dead. However, he might as well be. He is in prison serving a twenty-five year term for possession of drugs. He also had a gun in his possession when he was arrested. Since you left, Goldie, the only thing new in Harahan is an increasing drug problem and a new prison called the People's Prison Camp. That was supposed to be a temporary name. However, that name has remained. Everybody in town is ashamed of it. So, we refer to it as P.P.C. Delroy had several run ins with Sheriff Grimes. Sheriff Grimes had tried to work with him because of his friendship with Uncle Cyrus, but when Delroy got stopped for speeding on Long Beach Blvd he was clocked at ninety plus miles an hour. Personally, I think he was trying to kill himself. He does not want anybody to visit him in prison. I still go once a month. Aunt Beulah Mae went to see him once. She refuses to go anymore. Uncle Cyrus was the glue that held us together, Goldie. When he died we just fell apart. Aunt Beulah Mae tried in her own way to keep things going, but Delroy and I were not easy to handle. We never got real close to her. I know in her own way she loves us, but she has a difficult time expressing it. It was always so lively at your house. Uncle Yetis kept everybody laughing. Then there was the music. I loved coming over and listening to your aunt play the piano. Everybody also spoke what was on their mind. I remember the many discussions held right here in this kitchen. It was amazing how Uncle Yetis and Aunt Soya would listen to what you and the boys had to say about a matter. Then there were all the marvellous dishes that your aunt was always preparing. I enjoyed when she would invite me to help her out in the kitchen. You remember all the intereting stories your aunt and uncle would share with us about growing up in Harahan. Can you imagine meeting your soul mate in the cotton fields? It was always so quiet at Aunt Beulah Mae's. I guess that is why I had to stay busy cleaning and doing other household chores. I would recall how your aunt would be humming a tune as she did things around the house and I found myself doing the same thing. Actually, I grew to enjoy housekeeping. You can never complete all that needs to be done and so it was therapeutic for me. Now, enough about what has been going on in my life. I want to hear more about your ex-husband. I know you probably still feel something for Bomar. Actually, I was surprised to learn that you got married, but I was proud of the fact that you were trying to move on with your life."

"Dakota, before we talk about me, there was something else that your aunt said about my uncle."

"She didn't dare to tell you about Uncle Yetis' one night stand with that barroom hooker? My aunt has an amazing memory, but I assure you that what she implied was not true."

"Why is it that I am not aware of so many things that happened in the past, Dakota? No offense, but you are not even family."

"That's a matter of opinion, dear friend. Sometimes I have felt more a part of your family than my own, especially after you moved away. It was Uncle Yetis and Aunt Soya who kept me going after Uncle Cyrus died. And my failed marriage would have sent me over the edge if it were not for Uncle Yetis and Caleb. It was Uncle Yetis who convinced Emerson to allow me to have some association with my children. He had convinced the courts that I was an unfit mother. I had no money to fight back. My lawyer had convinced me that alimony was all that I could count on and she was not sure if it would be substantial. Caleb intervened at that point. I don't know the details of what transpired, but the outcome was to my advantage.

As for any discretion on the part of your uncle, I am sure you know that he would not do anything to deliberately hurt Aunt Soya. My understanding of the story is that a hooker tried to claim that Uncle Yetis was the father of her unborn child. However, your Aunt Soya nipped that in the bud. It turned out that the hooker was spreading a rumor that your uncle had gotten her pregnant. Little did she know that shortly after Caleb was born your uncle became almost deathly ill due to a very unusual virus that in the end rendered him with no sperm count. I think it is called some type of azoospermia. In the beginning, your aunt made Doc Worthington promise not to tell Uncle Yetis. He always wanted one more child in hopes of having a daughter. Your aunt felt that she would tell him at a later time and wow did she have to let that cat out of the bag. Anyway, back to this hooker incident. The hooker had intentionally gotten your uncle drunker after he left Bubba Dave's bar where they met. She invited him to come inside her apartment after he gave her a ride home. She had told Uncle Yetis when he came outside of the bar that her roommate had become angry at her and left her stranded. Uncle Yetis was hanging out with Mr. Joey Barber that night. Mr. Barber went on his way when Uncle Yetis got with the hooker. Upon entering her apartment, the roommate and the hooker, Ms Charolelette, insisted that Uncle Yetis remain for a few more drinks. The result was that Uncle Yetis passed out on the living room couch. He woke up at 7 a.m. the next morning. The hooker and her roommate were gone. Uncle Yetis had no clue what had happen. He knew he needed to come up with an explanation for Aunt Soya. In the end, he decided to tell her the truth. The details of that encounter have yet to be revealed, but I was told that when the rumor starting circulating about three months later that this hooker was pregnant by your uncle, Aunt Soya was one angry woman. She was able to get the truth out of them when she showed up at their apartment one day with Sheriff Grimes and Mr. Gant, Sr. Did you know that besides being the founder and owner of Gant's Oil and Refinery, Mr. Gant, Sr. is a graduate of Harvard Law School. Anyway, they frighten those two women to the extent that they left town by the next morning. Unfortunately, your aunt waited until this incident occurred before telling your uncle about his condition."

"Do my cousins know the truth, Dakota?"

"Yes, they do, Goldie."

"I suppose that my aunt felt that Uncle Yetis would not have been able to handle not having any more children at that time."

"Well, Goldie, it was a little more complicated than that. It seems that your aunt was trying to protect her marriage in light of the fact that she had another child about two years after Caleb was born. The little girl lived for two to three days. I do not remember the correct number of days. Your Uncle's encounter with the hooker happened about a year later."

Goldie felt her head spinning. Then she recalled when she was around 10 years old, Uncle Yetis walked her home from school one fall day. He had told her that they were going to take a short cut through the cemetery which was within a short walking distance of the elementary school's campus. He had told her she should never be afraid of the dead and to always pray in their behalf the same as for the living. She was excited and curious about the walk through. She could hardly wait to tell Dakota about this adventure. She was already planning for the two of them to bravely return to the cemetery on their own. Uncle Yetis showed her the graves of family members and friends. He shared some minor details about the circumstances of most of their deaths. Finally, he showed her a very small grave in the farthest left corner of the cemetery. It was well maintained. It appeared someone had recently put fresh flowers around it. Uncle Yetis informed her that it was the grave of the daughter that he never had. The grave marker simply said "Elycia Miriam—born Feb. 2. 1957, died Feb. 4, 1957." Goldie noticed that her uncle appeared to be somewhat emotional and he stood quietly before the grave with his hands behind him and his eyes closed. His headed was tilted upward. She had wanted more information about Elycia, but her uncle remained silent. She stood silently beside him and reached for his hand. He grasped her hand tightly. When he finally let go, she was relieved and then he escorted her out of the cementary. She told Dakota about the visit to the grave yard, but she had never shared that moment with Dakota.

"Tell me Dakota, when I showed you the grave of the newborn baby girl did you know anything about her?"

"No, I did not at the time. But I did tell Aunt Beulah about it later. I had never seen a grave so tiny. I asked her if a child was really buried in it. She told me yes. She also told me that your aunt had given birth to the baby girl in the grave."

"But how could my aunt have given birth to a child at that time? She was born after Caleb."

"Goldie, your uncle shared somethings with me a few weeks before he died. He told me when I felt the time was right to tell you. I was not planning to discuss anything with you until I believed you were stronger considering your uncle's recent demise."

"But, why did my uncle tell you, Dakota and not me?"

"That is another one of those questions that I can not answer, Goldie. Perhaps as you reflect on matters at a later time, you will have an "Ah, Ha" moment. Just promise me that you will not tell your aunt that I told you. Your uncle loved your aunt more than anyone or anything else in this world. When she was raped, it almost destroyed him."

"Raped?" Goldie spoke with ambivalence. Perhaps she should end this discussion; however she felt that Uncle Yetis wanted her to finally learn the truth about family matters that had been kept from her. She was feeling anxious, but she decided to let her friend continue. "Dakota, I never knew anything about my aunt being raped which meant my Aunt did not have an affair."

"Of course, Aunt Soya did not have an affair. That's the rumor that surfaced. People should mine their own business. Your aunt loved Uncle Yetis as much as he loved her. Those two were meant to be. I hope you and I will find a man like your uncle in the near future."

"Stay focus, Dakota. I know what it is to have a good man. You just have to be sure that he is the right one for you. I am glad to know the truth, finally. There seems to have been a lot of collusion going on in my family. A lot more than what was going on with my parents."

Dakota watched her friend more intensely. Revealing family secrets was no easy task. She had more information to tell her dear friend. She had promised Uncle Yetis that she would not hold back anything.

'Goldie, I know who raped your aunt. Your uncle told me to tell you because there are so many rumors floating around town. I must confess that this is difficult for me."

Goldie was not sure if she was ready to learn who the rapist could be. She wondered if he was still alive. She decided to not speculate and just allow Dakota to tell her what she needed to know. Poor Uncle Yetis, she thought, had to be devasted by this incident.

Reluctantly, Dakota informed her friend that the rapist was Mr. Emerson Gant, Sr. She watched as Goldie's entire facial expression changed. She appeared to be in a state of shock. She wanted to say more, but decided to wait for some type of cue from Goldie to know if she could continue.

Goldie found her whole body stiffening as the name of the rapist was revealed. She discontinued eye contact with Dakota. She felt as though the wind had been knocked out of her. She knew Dakota was trying to wait on her before sharing the details of what happened. She was beginning to understand the inner turmoil that her uncle must have been dealing with. Sometimes, she had felt that her aunt also had a sense of hopelessness about helping her uncle overcome his drinking. The two were sharing a pain that would forever haunt them.

"Goldie, I will give you some of the details of this unfortunate situation as related to me by your uncle. It seems that in your uncle's earlier days he had a gambling problem. Your aunt was eventually contacted by two hired ruffians of Mr. Harrison York, the owner of the only nightspot in town at the time. The two showed up at the church one Sunday just as service was beginning to get started. They approached Aunt Soya before she entered and informed her that she would have to go with them. Of course, she had no clue what was going on, but she realized she needed to cooperate with the two scabs. They took her to Mr. York. Mr. York informed her that Uncle Yetis had accrued a debt of over $10,000. 00 and he expected to be paid within seven days. He told her he was tired of wasting his time with Uncle Yetis and since she had a reputation for being a reasonable and smart woman that she would see to getting him his money. Your aunt did not tell your uncle about this incident in the beginning. She decided to approach Mr. Gant, Sr. about loaning her the money."

"Why did she choose Mr Gant and not the bank, Dakota?

"It seems that before your aunt met Uncle Yetis, she knew Mr. Gant, Sr. He had been attracted to her when they were in the jr. high school. However, his family did not approve of their dating. I am sure that I do not need to explain why. Anyway, your aunt was feeling desperate. She did not believe she could borrow that kind of money from the bank. She was willing to take out a second mortgage on their house and land, but she did not feel the bank would act within a week. By the third day after the threat, she felt she had no option but to approach Mr. Emerson Gant, Sr. She contacted him at his office and he told her to come by that day. She showed up at 11 a.m. She had decided to dress up in her Sunday attire with her hair down. You know Aunt Soya is a very attractive woman although she seems to do her best to cover herself up. She got my Uncle Cyrus to drop her off at Mr Gant's Office. She did not realize that his secretary would be at lunch. Also, she had not discerned that he had been drinking when she called. When she arrived, she told my uncle she would get a cab when she was ready to leave. Although Mr. Gant met her at the door, she did not suspect anything. She was able to explain the purpose of her visit. He agreed to loan her the money. He would go with her the next day to meet with Mr. York. Your aunt was so relieved that she failed to notice that as she was preparing to leave, he was suddenly grabbing for her. She thought he was getting up to the open the door for her to exit. She could then smell the liquor on him as she tried to resist him. She fought him like a cat that was cornered. But it was to no avail. That man's six feet, three inches frame towered over her. He was able to cover her mouth to keep her from screaming. She was crying and trying to muffle," No!" He threw her on the office sofa and she realized she could not get away unless she killed him. Afterwards, he apologized and told her he did not realize what had gotten into him. He told her that he had always been in love with her and that he would not fight her if she brought charges against him. Your aunt was so ashamed. She felt perhaps she had tempted him. She never should have stayed when she discovered his secretary was not there. She was too distraught to call a cab and she wanted to leave before the secretary returned. She insisted that Mr. Gant, Sr. take her to see Dr. Worthington. He cooperated with her and even went inside with her. Dr. Worthington had agreed to see her immediately. They entered through a back door. Dr. Worthington insisted on calling the police before he examined her, but Aunt Soya refused to do that and pleaded with the doctor to let her handle matters. Dr. Worthington reluctantly went along with Aunt Soya's request. He also promised that he would tell no one."

Goldie recalled the close relationship that Dr. Worthington and her aunt had. He was like a father to her. He died before Goldie graduated from high school. She had noticed how devasted her aunt had been over his passing. She had visited him often with her aunt after he retired from his medical practice. To her knowledge, he was never married and did not have any children. Her aunt would often say that he suddenly appeared in Harahan one day and opened up his medical practice which was very much needed. He was a genuinely caring, giving and passionate man. The entire town of Harahan loved him. The ladies made sure that his house was cleaned and someone always prepared meals for him. The men in the community kept his yard cut and his home was never allowed to fall into disrepair. This display of generosity continued even after he retired from his practice. After one of his patient's husband died from injuries due to a stabbing, he took the young lady and her son in shortly after he retired. She took care of him as his health failed and he left everything to her and her son.

"So are you saying that my aunt did become pregnant as a result of the rape, Dakota?"

"Yes she did, Goldie. She had decided she would keep the child and raise it as though Uncle Yetis was the father. Your uncle was not aware at this time that he could not father a child. However, the baby was born six months prematurely and only lived three days. Your aunt was devastated. She felt God was punishing her. She also had not told your uncle the truth. He was looking forward to the birth of this child which turned out to be a girl. Shortly after this, the incident with the prostitutes occurred. That is when your aunt realized she would have to tell Uncle Yetis about his inability to father any more children and the rape. She took Uncle Yetis to see Dr. Worthington and the doctor confirmed everything."

Goldie felt that nothing about life was perspicuous at that moment. She was always reaching for the stars and wanting something more. Everything had always centered around her and what she wanted. She never assumed anybody's life was more complicated than hers. And to borrow one of her aunt's favorite comments, everything about her life was "moot". Her aunt and uncle had been very self-sacrificing and protective of her. She now understood Uncle Yetis' secret torment. He had tried to go along with the way Aunt Soya had handled matters. Often life is never as it seems. Smiling faces were the biggest cover up.

"Goldie, do not try to be judgemental of your aunt and uncle. They did what they thought was best at the time. Your uncle wanted you to know the truth about matters in case you decided to move back home to Harahan one day."

Suddenly, Aunt Soya appeared in the kitchen unexpectedly. She noticed Dakota's abrupt silence and how Goldie stared at her almost sympathetically. Still exhausted from the long day, she sat quietly at the table. She suspected whatever they were talking about involved her.

Goldie broke the silence. "Aunt Soya", she said in a very calm manner, "why did you not bring charges against Mr. Gant, Sr. How could you have allowed Uncle Yetis to be tormented all these years?"

Aunt Soya looked indignantly at Dakota. "Not today, child", she spoke almost through clenched teeth.

I do not ever expect you to understand my reasons for taking the actions that I did. But, I want you to know that some things can never be undone once they occur. I had a situation that happened to me. I also knew that all the law enforcement in the world could never take the pain and humiliation that I suffered away from me. They could also never take away the pain that my husband would feel. I decided that there were other options for me than to simply have Mr. Gant, Sr. locked up in jail. With the money that his family had, I was not sure that he might spend one day in jail. What you probably do not know is that Mr. Gant still insisted on giving me the money to get my Yetis out of that gambling debt. He also expunged all of our indebtedness to him. You see, that was not the first time that I had borrowed money from Mr. Gant. I decided why not let this man clear all the money that we owed him. Mr. Gant was a rich and powerful man. His family owns most of the land in Harahan and they have been involved in so many businesses getting off the grown. In light of what happened, Gant Sr. became a changed man to a certain extent. He offered to pay for both of my sons to go to college. He paid off the remaining mortgage of our home. He also made an undisclosed contribution to the church. You might find this difficult to understand, but I also knew that in the context of the law that Mr. Gant had raped me, it was still not totally about controll. Dispite his drunken state, when I momentarily looked in his eyes, I could tell that in his own crazy way he loved me. I on the other hand, had no feelings whatsoever for him. As he raped me, I felt contempt. I had decided for the first time in my life that I was personally going to kill another human being. I just did not did not know how or when. After he molested me, he looked me directly in the eyes and I started crying again uncontrollablely. He tried to speak, but his mouth would not form words. I could tell he was aware of my hurt and my anger. He started crying and telling me that he was sorry. He got up and left the room. He returned shortly and told me he would cooperate with whatever I wanted to do. I told him to take me to Dr. Worthington's office. He cooperated and went inside with me through a back entrance. He confessed to Dr. Worthington. Dr. Worthington became so angry at him that I thought he might attack him. I had to step in between them. Dr. Worthington kept threatening to call the police. But I begged and pleaded with him not to do that. Then Dr. Worthington insisted that Mr. Gant leave his office. I was able to clean up and get myself together. I stayed in the back until Dr. Worthington's last patient for the day had gone. Dr. Worthington called Yetis and told him that I had gotten sick and stopped by his office. He was watching over me to make sure that I got better. Yetis had insisted on coming to get me, but the doctor told him he was dropping me off. On the way home, I again reminded the doctor not to report the incident to the police or inform Yetis about what had happened."

"But Aunt Soya, how could you not think about the impact that everything would have on Uncle Yetis? "Goldie was trying to not be angry at her aunt.

"It was my body, Goldie. I decided it would be more of an ego thing for Yetis. I knew his love for me would cause him to re-act instead of think the whole matter through. If it had not been for the hooker incident, I might have been able to spare Yetis so much hurt. He went along with my decision despite the fact that he was not in agreement with me. For a while, I felt that he might consider killing Mr. Gant. I would not allow him to inform the boys. I threaten to leave him if he did. I insisted that they must be spared any knowledge of the rape. I grew to realize how I set a chain of inner torture for that man that eventually made a wedge in our relationship that nearly destroyed our love. But, my Yetis really loved me. The last few months that we shared together, he often told me that he never was in agreement with the way I handled matters, but he realized I had to be the one to decide what should be done. He said that on several occasions, he had seriously considered killing Mr. Gant, but he realized nothing could undo what had been done. That always troubled him, but he finally had to let the anger and hate go. If he had acted on his emotions who knows what our lives would have been like moving forward into the future. Just having me still in his life became his focus. He told me that before he came home from the hospital Mr. Gant visited him. He again apologized for what had happened. He admitted that he had come to realize that Yetis and I truly loved each other, unconditionally. He said that he had even entertained the thought that Yetis might leave me when he learned about the rape. Yetis said he actually cried and asked him to please forgive him. He said Yetis was a lucky man to have married me. He even offered to pay for Yetis' funeral, but I said no. And now, young ladies, please excuse me. I am going to bed and I plan to sleep peacefully."

Both Goldie and Dakota simply nodded their heads in agreement as Aunt Soya got up from the table.

Goldie dismissed the urge to give her a hug. Suddenly, her thoughts were interrupted by the sound of Dakota's voice.

"I will understand if you want to retreat for the night, Goldie. According to that clock on the stove behind you, it's almost 10:30 p.m. I am enjoying being with you. We have so much catching up to do. I would love to stop by in the morning and take you to breakfast. There is a poplar spot for our age group that is known for their fabulous breakfast buffet. Hopefully, you can tell me about your marriage and fill me in on what happen between you and Bomar. You know I never forgave you for just leaving me without an explanation. You simply distanced yourself and then took that job offer out of town."

"Actually, hearing Aunt Soya's explanation of what happen in the past has made me more awake. It would be a restless sleep for me if I retired right now. But I need to hear more from you about your appearance at my uncle's funeral. I heard you made a grand entrance."

"Since you were at Aunt Beulah's house before you came back here, I know she must of have told you something. I had intended to remain outside until you showed up and enter with you. However, after about thirty minutes had passed, I concluded that you might not make the funeral. I decided to go on inside and sit next to your aunt on the front row. There was still enough space if you arrived. I was trying to be as inconspicuous as possible. Although, my decision to dress in all white did not imply that. I just could not bring myself to wear any dark colors to your Uncle Yetis' funeral. Despite all these revelations about the past, I saw him as a very lively person. Even when he was drunk, there was a twinkle in his eyes. He often told me that he thought I looked very lovely in white. I was trying not to be disrespectful."

"Dakota, you and I have been very stubborn about taking advice when it comes to the men in our lives. I'm divorced from Randall. He was a wonderful, loving and kind human being that I did not deserve. I am experiencing a lot of guilt about the pain I must have put him through. I did love him, but I should never have married him. I realized despite the passing of several years, it was still a rebound from my break-up with Bomar. Even though, I learned to live without Bomar, I never stopped loving him. Poor Randall, he really tried to make our marriage work. He finally told me one morning that he was just tired of living in another man's shadow. We were married for five years."

"That is terrible, my friend. And to think, I have not been there for you. I might as well tell you that Bomar was at the funeral. He did not go inside. I saw him drive up shortly after the funeral started. I walked over to his car to speak to him. He asked me if you were there and I told him no. He said thanks and drove away."

"Dakota, so your aunt was right when she said he was back in Harahan."

"Well, I am not suppose to tell you anything according to your aunt. She never counted on you visiting so soon with my aunt. Anyway, Bomar returned to Harahan about three months ago. He visited your Uncle Yetis several times before his passing. He has opened up the first photography shop in Harahan. He's doing quite well. Mr. Gant, Sr. sponsored a grand opening for him. I have not gone by his shop. I have watched him from a distance. I will tell you he still looks the same with those droopy eyes. You know, I believe that man still aches for you. I can see it in his face."

As Dakota spoke, Goldie thought about her first encounter with Bomar. Her aunt had said later after meeting Bomar that she had never heard of a man named Bomar. As far as she was concerned there was something not right about that name. Nevertheless, that man named Bomar stole her niece's heart. Caleb and Greer tried to tell their mother that Baby Sistah had fallen in love and for her there was no "other". Goldie remembered her encounter with Bomar at the college campus. She could still picture him in her mine as he walked hurriedly across the campus quad. He was overloaded with his photography equipment. He was tall and took long strides. She had been bicycling with some girlfriends. They were securing their bikes in order to rush to the Commons Hall for dinner. She noticed Bomar dropped something as he walked.

She told her friends to go on inside without her. She rushed to pick up the item that Bomar had dropped. She hoped she would be able to catch up with him. He exited between the two dorm buildings that faced the parking lot. She was almost out of breath when she caught up with him. He was in his car backing out of the parking space. She was yelling for him to wait up as she jumped in front of the car waving what turned out to be camera lens. He had been looking in his rear view mirror when he suddenly became aware of her shouting and jumping in front his car. He stopped backing up and started letting his driverside window down. She approached it holding out the lens for him to see in her hand. He put the car in park again and got out. He obtained the lens from her and thanked her. Goldie had not realized just how handsome this man was until she was standing close by him. She felt an immediate attraction. She did not want to give him direct eye contact. She could tell he had to be in his early twenties. He had a more mature look about him than most of the guys on campus. He appeared to be surprised that he had dropped the lens.

"I did not realize that I dropped the lens, Ms._____?" was Bomar's initial response.

He waited for Goldie to tell him her name. He found himself scrutinizing her more closely. She had a very refreshing look about her that he found very attractive. He could tell she was several years younger than his 27 years. He actually hoped that she did not perceive him as much older. He assumed his dress might give it away. He was neither the college preppy type or the Ivy League type. He had dressed in a white T-Shirt and casual blue jeans. He had decided to take pictures of the campus which he found to be impressively landscaped. He had not shaved. Being new to the area, he did not expect to run into anyone that he knew.

Suddenly, the Commons Hall bell rang for the last dinner round.

Goldie exclaimed that she must get back to the hall or she would miss dinner. Then she realized she had not told him her name.

"My name is Marigold, she interjected. But, you can call me Goldie like all my friends do."

"Mine is Bomar, Bomar Henderson. Thank you for returning my lens. They are a very expensive item to replace. I would love to reward you with an offer of dinning with me." Bomar immediately felt that perhaps he was too forward. After all, he was still a perfect stranger. She was only doing a good deed by returning his lens.

Goldie was somewhat surprised at the invitation, but she was thrilled that he had asked. She quickly responded with a, "Yes I would like that." She felt that Bomar was trustworthy and the strong attraction that she was feeling would not let her just simply walk away. He opened the passenger side door for her. As she got into the car, she kept repeating the name Bomar in her head. She liked the sound of that name and that man's voice. Bomar was the only man with the voice that could just reach out and touch her.

Three and a half thrilling and wonderful years of Bomar being in her life came and ended. She moved in with him immediately after graduating from college. Aunt Soya was just sick about it. She tried so hard to tell Goldie to slow down. Yes things were moving too fast and Goldie loved every moment it. Bomar was her world. She sensed a quiet side to him at times. However Goldie never pursued it. She found him to be very supportive of her and her career interest. In the end the two of them just blended.

Goldie also loved Bomar's work. He had convinced her to let him take many photo shots of her. His pictures were always very flattering. He was able to take photos of Uncle Yetis and Aunt Soya that were just incredible in the way he captured their very essence. As time passed, Uncle Yetis and Aunt Soya grew to be more accepting of him. Aunt Soya realized that Bomar really loved her. However, Aunt Soya would always tell her that she was troubled about his views regarding God. Goldie tried to avoid the subject as much as possible. Bomar had told her that as a child his parents did not insist that he go to church. They told him that God existed in everybody and that God was always accessible without any one else having to intervene on their behalf. She never questioned this view point but she appreciated that he would occasionally attend church with her just too quiet Aunt Soya, who secretly referred to him as a heathen. Goldie actually found it amusing because she felt Bomar went to church more than Uncle Yetis and the boys. After she moved in with Bomar, Aunt Soya wanted to know why they were not at least engaged. Goldie was just too happy with the way things were. She was convinced that marriage was inevitable for them. Then one day Bomar called her at work and told her that he had to fly immediately to Scotland. His voice was shaky and he sounded so distant to her. He did manage to tell her that his wife and daughter had been stabbed by her boyfriend. "His wife! What wife?" she thought. She could barely understand Bomar as he tearfully told her that he would be in touch after he got to Scotland.

Bomar called her after a three day absence. It had seemed like an eternity to Goldie. He tried to reveal as much as he could over the phone. He told her he had wanted to discuss things face to face with her, but because he was still legally married to Bridgette he had to remain in Scotland to manage some of her affairs. He stated he estimated he would be gone for the next 30 days. Goldie felt like she was being stabbed in the heart as Bomar told her he and his wife had separated after nine months of marriage. His wife of thirteen years was stabbed to death by her lover. He also stabbed the daughter, but it appeared that she was going to survive. The child was fathered by Bridgett's lover. When the police arrived on the scene, the lover shot himself to death. Bomar managed to tell her that when Bridgett informed him that she was three months pregnant, after one and ½ months of marriage he knew he could not be the father because they had never been sexually involved prior to their marriage. He had told her he would quietly moved out and let her tell their parents what was going on. However, Bridgette had begged him to stay with her until after the baby was born. She could not handle moving back home with her overbearing parents. Bridgette also stated that she would never agree to a divorce or admit to anyone that he was not the father. Six months after the child was born he moved out. He told Bridgette that he would soon be moving to the United States. Because the baby looked so much like Bridgette, he agreed to keep quiet about the real father. Both sets of parents adored the child who Bridgette named Erikka, after the real father, Erik Conard. Bomar informed Goldie that he had married Bridgette after his senior year in high school. Their parents were very protective and insisted on this pre-arranged marriage. Bomar admitted that he found Bridgette to be very attractive, but he despised her personality. She was a very spoiled and selfish rich girl whose parents simply adored her. His father was a retired US Airforce Lieutenant and his mother was an art teacher. They decided to live in Scotland permanently after his father was station there for three years. They fell in love with the country and the people. He told her he had wanted to tell her about Bridgette in the beginning when they first met. He called Bridgette after his encounter with Goldie on the college campus. He told her he wanted a divorce and to come clean about Erikka's father. Bridgette had told him to give her a little more time. She and Erik were in fact planning to get married and she wanted to wait until after the marriage to tell them that Erik was the real father. Erik had bought her an engagement ring. She was planning to file for divorce in the next couple of weeks. One week later Bridgette had called him back. She said she was not going to be divorcing him. She wanted to come to the U.S. with Erikka. She stated Erik had threatened to beat her again after she had asked him to leave the apartment. He had come home in the early hours of the morning extremely intoxicated. When she confronted him and asked him where had he been all night, he reached out and slapped her several times. She called the police. They took him away. She decided this was the last straw and she needed to get away from him. He had suggested that she should move back in with her parents for awhile. Now he was feeling guilty about discouraging her to move to the States. In addition, he realized he would have to inform the grandparents the truth about Erikka's father.

What was supposed to be a one month absence, turned into a six months absence. Goldie moved out of Bomar's apartment and back in with her aunt and uncle at the end of the second month that Bomar was gone. He tried calling Goldie at least once a week to keep her informed about matters. Bridgette's parents were going to raise Erikka and his parents stated they would continue to be part of her life as long as Bridgette's parents allowed it. Erikka was making a full recovery from her stabbing injuries. She was a good child. She only resembled her mother in looks. Bridgette had a sizable estate to be handled. She was actually an astute business woman. She had made several investments that proved to be very lucrative. A very prominent law firm was able to help Bomar settle her estate in a manner that was equitable for him and Erikka.

His guilt continued to weigh heavily on him. After the third month, his calls to Goldie suddenly stopped.

Aunt Soya and Uncle Yetis welcomed Goldie back home with open arms. They gave her space. No discussions were held. They were concerned when Goldie informed them that she was applying for jobs out of town shortly after moving in with them. She stated Harahan was beginning to make her feel smothered. Two months after moving in with her aunt and uncle again, she got the job offer from Vaccarro Del Belle. Uncle Yetis was very excited for her, but Aunt Soya was not favourable to the idea of her baby girl moving away. However, she told Goldie that she would not hold her back and stated that she would let her go with her blessings. She decided to give Goldie a going away party.

A month after Goldie left town, Bomar returned. He had been gone six months. He could not believe that Goldie had accepted a job offer away from Harahan. Nobody would tell him how to get in touch with her. Aunt Soya and Uncle Yetis felt it was for the best. Even Dakota refused to talk to him. How was he going to continue on without Goldie? The legal matters had dragged on longer than he thought they would. Also, his parents were having a difficult time after learning the truth about everything. He decided he needed to stay longer to be with them. He had tried to explain all of this the last time he had spoken with Goldie. She had told him to stop calling her and handle his business. He decided that she needed time to digest everything. He would be patient. Surely she knew that he loved her and now he could marry her.

"Goldie, Dakota said trying to get her friend's attention. You have got to see Bomar. You can not make the same mistake twice. How many people get a second chance to be with their soulmate?"

"I thought you did not think he was right for me, Dakota"

"That was then and this is now as the old folks say. Besides, since when did either of us care what others felt about the man in our life. I must admit that I never understood why you totally let Bomar go after his wife died. He was a free man."

"I can not quite explain it myself, Dakota. Perhaps it was pride. How could he have kept his marriage a secret from me during our entire relationship? He did tell me that his parents lived in Scotland and that he was an only child. I loved and trusted that man so very very much. I thought I knew every inch of his mind and body."

The sudden ringing of the front door bell caught both women by surprised. It was about 11:15 p. m. Dakota jumped up and said she was going to spend the night with Aunt Beulah Mae. Caleb was shouting that he would get the door. Godlie was contemplating walking Dakota half way to her aunt's when suddenly Caleb appeared in the kitchen with the late night visitor. She and Dakota were speechless. Both were surprised to see that it was Bomar.

Caleb grabbed Dakota by the hand and informed her that he would escort her to her aunt's home.

Dakota did no object.

Goldie could not believe she was in the same room with Bomar. She remained seated because she felt she would loose her composure if she stood up. She also could not believe the affect that he was having on her after wat had to be close to 6 years. Her heart was racing. She could only look at him.

Bomar was the first to speak.

"Goldie, I know it is very late. But I called Caleb before I came. He told me you were still up. I really needed to see you and talk briefly with you. I have deeply regretted not being honest with you. After your uncle died, I could only think about the fact that you would be here for the funeral. Your uncle told me a few days before he died that you were divorced."

Bomar was trying to make sure that he said the right things to her. Seeing her in the bright kitchen light gave him such pleasure. He realized he was swelling up with desire for her the way he had always felt toward her. This woman was still able to stir up emotions in him that he had tried to forget, although he was often dreaming about her. He had no desire to get to know anyone else. He had felt that they had some unresolved issues to settle.

"I know why you did not pursue divorcing Bridgette, Bomar. Uncle Yetis told me when I last visited him. He said it was because of the money. You even married her because f her family's money."

"That's true, Goldie. Our parents pushed us into a relationship and insisted that we get married. They started planning it while we were in junior high school. Our parents had developed a very close relationship. I was an only child and so was Bridgette. I was her escort to most of her social functions. Despite her attractive looks, I never developed a real fondness for her. I was beginning to develop an interest in photography. However, my confidence was almost non-existence. I felt that if I did not succeed as a professional photographer that at least I would have money to fall back on. I have lived to regret my decision, but I was young and inexperienced. I always was somewhat materialistic. Then, I met you and nothing else mattered. I just wanted to be free from Bridgette to be with you.

Goldie listened quietly and attentively as Bomar looked endearingly into her eyes. She could tell that Uncle Yetis had been busy with trying to get his affairs and every body else's affairs in order his last few weeks on this earth. She felt a calmness coming over her. She put both of her hands together and said a silent prayer of thanks to Uncle Yetis. Then she got up from the table while Bomar watched her in a questioning silence. She looked him boldy in the eyes. "It's getting to be one of those 24 hour days, Bomar. You had better come back tomorrow."

Bomar dared himself to take, Goldie in his arms. As he looked into her eyes, he could see that 18 years old college girl that had ran to give him his camera lens. This time she was giving him something more valuable, her love and her trust. He reached out and pulled her to him. Uncle Yetis had been right. She still cared deeply for him. He would not disappoint her this time. He could feel her passion. She offered no resistance as he kissed her gently on her soft lips. He let her go after a few moments. Maybe she would stay in Harahan and accept the superintendent of Schools position that the former classmates were prepared to offer her. He had to believe that Uncle Yetis was right when he said she was always headed back to Harahan. This place was her true roots.

Goldie awaken the next morning to sunlight streaming through her bedroom window from opened curtains that she was sure were closed when she went to bed. She was feeling very rested. As she slowly opened her eyes, she realized her Aunt Soya was sitting at the foot of the bed. She was looking directly at Goldie and smiling in a manner that Goldie had not seen for quite some time. Goldie began positioning herself to sit up and say something, but her aunt put a finger on her right hand to her lips signaling Goldie to be quiet.

"Goldie, there is something that I must share with you before you go down stairs to meet with everyone. I have been sitting here watching you as you slept. I have something that I must share with you. I will begin by telling you how much I love you and how very proud I am of you. You have filled a void in my life and the life of this family. You are the daughter that Yetis and always wanted. Yetis was right when he said you were the little seedling that grew into a beautiful flower and brought joy to this house. You were a self-rising flower, caring, loving and giving all the time."

Goldie was totally speechless as she listened and looked intently at her aunt. She was somewhat in awe of her aunt's almost radiant appearance as she sat on the bed wearing a golden yellow smock. She found herself opening and closing her eyes to make sure she was not dreaming as she stared at her aunt.

"Do not interrupt me as I share something very important with you my precious little sunshine. It seems that my time on this earth is also winding down. You know how much I miss Yetis. So that is infact good news for me as far as I am concerned. Young Dr. Madison has done all he can to keep me holding on. My only concern has been for you and the boys. Since my Yetis left me behind, I know it will be very difficult in the beginning for you all to deal with another death. But shortly after I retired for bed last night Yetis appeared to me. He was sitting at the foot of my bed just as I am sitting at yours. He was smiling lovingly at me. He told me he was at peace and everything was alright. He wanted me to tell you that you should not be troubled because you missed the funeral services. He said to be sure and tell you that funerals are for the living. Then he stood up and moved closer to me kissing me on my forehead. I smelled the scent of that cologne that you sent him for Christmas one year. You said that nice Mr. Napoleon had recommended it. When I woke up this morning, this note was on my night stand. It is in Yetis' scribbled hand writing."

Goldie took the note from her aunt's hand. It was definitely her uncle's hand writing. The note simply read, "Dear Soya, I will see you soon. Love Yetis." Goldie could also smell the scent of her uncle's cologne on the note. She recalled during her last visit that Uncle Yetis had told her that he had used up all of the cologne and he wanted her to send him some more. She had completely forgotten to follow up on his request.

"Goldie, I do not want you fretting over what I have shared with you. This means you will not share it with the boys. Now, my dear, I want you to know about the chest in the left corner of my bedroom closet. It contains important papers and my will. It also has information about my funeral arrangement. I know you can handle this. I am going to leave so that you can get up and get dressed. You have so much to learn today."

Goldie turned to look at the radio clock on the nightstand next to her bed as her aunt exited the room. She was surprised to see that it was 11:00 a. m. She immediately jumped out of the bed and headed straight for the shower. She was dressed in about twenty minutes. Her aunt's appearance in her room created some mixed feeling about the forthcoming day. What else could she learn that she did not already know about? She could hear lots of talking and laughter as she approached the top of the stairs. As she descended the stairs, a familiar voice from the past called up to her. She was feeling very anxious as she approached the last step. Now, standing there quietly and watching her every move was her father, Drake. She was certain that it was him. He had the same deep set brown eyes and thick black eyebrows with some grey hairs. He still had a full head of hair mingled with black and grey strands. His slightly crooked smile was more difficult for her discern because he had grown a very thick grey and black moustache which she decided she liked. He had gained wait over the years, but she felt it suited him. He looked more mature and fatherly. When he reached out to hug her, she did not resist in any way. Then, he let her go as fast as he had grabbed for her. He was motioning for someone else to approach them. The woman was in a wheelchair. As Goldie watched her movement toward them, she knew in an instant that it was Gwenetta. By now the house had become very quiet. Gwenetta without warning held her arms out to Goldie. Goldie, like a little child hastily moved closer and bending down she allowed her mother to gently hug her. Goldie thought she smelled good. She could tell it was an expensive perfume. As she slowly pulled away from her mother, she found herself staring at her. Seeing Gwenetta in a wheel chair was somewhat difficult for to accept. She felt Gwenetta was still very attractive. Her hair length was longer. Goldie was surprised that she did not cover up the grey. Her make up appeared to have been professionally done. Goldie felt her attire was very flattering. Her fingernails were well manicured. Goldie concluded she had the appearance of a classy woman who led an opulent life style. Oddly enough, she found herself thinking about Ms. Bland as she continued quietly gazing at her.

Goldie had always thought that her encounter with her parents after all these years would be confrontational. When the tears started rolling down her cheeks, she felt a need to get away and be alone.

However, Gwenetta started crying softly. Goldie reached down and hugged her again. By now, she was also crying. Finally, Drake pulled them apart. He was very emotional, but he was able to hold back the tears. He roled Gwenetta into the living room as Goldie walked by his side. He asked Goldie to sit by him on the couch. She thought about the day when he had sat by her on the swing to say goodbye when she was six years old. Could they just pick up the pieces and start a new life together? With Aunt Soya talking about dying and the loss of Uncle Yetis, she was going to need someone to replace them.

"Goldie, your mother and I want to ask you to forgive us for being away from you all these years. I am not making any excuses for not returning to Harahan to to get you. It was not an easy decision to leave you. I did have good feelings about the fact that we left you with my sister and her family."

Goldie was wondering if she was finally going to learn more details about why her parents did not come back for her. Like a little girl, she leaned her head on Drakes shoulder. She had always felt closer to him as a child growing up. He began telling her that he and Gwenetta were involved in a car accident the same day they left her. They were about 100 miles outside of Harahan. The accident resulted in a very substantial financial settlement for him and Gwenetta.

Gwenetta sustained severe injuries in both of her legs. He made a full recovery. However, Gwenetta was unable to walk. She would require a personal assistant, but Gwenetta would not cooperate with anyone but him. This ended his plans to work outside of the home. They asked Aunt Soya to not tell Goldie anything until they knew the long term impact of Gwenetta's injuries. They visited doctors all over the country hoping for some good news that she would one day walk again, but unfortunately that was not going to happen. When Gwenetta had to accept the fact that she would never walk again, she insisted that she did not want Goldie to come back and live with a mother who was disabled. She argued with Drake about letting her remain with his sister's family. Drake eventually gave in to her wishes. In the meanwhile, they were able to send money to Aunt Soya to provide for all of Goldie's needs. They eventually learned that Aunt Soya was saving most of the money to fund Goldie's college education.

Goldie reflected back on how her aunt never complained about buying her anything related to school. Her aunt and uncle also bought her a car when she turned sixteen. When she insisted on working while she was in college, her aunt told her she needed to focus on her studies. She did win a full four year scholarship, but her aunt would send her a monthly allowance of $200 to $250 a month. Sometimes she wondered how they were able to afford the things that they did for her, but she was too busy enjoying her young life that she did not make a big issue of it. Since she was not hearing from her parents she assumed things were not good enough for her live with them. Besides, after a couple of years went by she decided she wanted to continue to live with her aunt and uncle. She never told anyone that she actually hoped Drake and Gwenetta would never return for her.

Drake continued to tell Goldie that he and Gwenetta had decided that they must attend Yetis' funneral and finally face her. When Goldie did not show for the funneral, they were actually somewhat relieved. They decided they would return home this morning without seeing her. However, Dakota and Caleb came by the hotel late last night and insisted that they owed it to Goldie to help her deal with Uncle Yetis' death.

Goldie had always admired how Dakota could convince people to do things that they had no intentions of doing. She was nevertheless amazed that she had that impact on her parents. She had never given much thought about her parents' attendance at the funeral. She had learned as a child to move on with her life. She had Aunt Soya and Uncle Yets to look after her. She always felt that they did a very good job.

"Goldie, honey, there is something else that your mother wants to tell you." Drake said with some hesitancy. Goldie watched as Gwenetta rolled her wheel chair toward the book shelf by the fire place. She pulled out a large Bible. Goldie recognized it immediately. It was the one that belonged to Ms. Bland. Her mother asked her if she remembered the Bible. Goldie remained quiet and simply nodded her head up and down. Gwenetta opened the Bible and then removed an envelope that looked faded. She handed the envelop to Goldie. And much to Goldie's surprised; the envelope had her name on the front of it. There was no return address. The envelope was still sealed although the glue had lost some of its stickiness. Goldie felt her hands begin to tremble as she opened the envelope. She wondered how she missed seeing the large Bible on the bookcase all these years. Gwenetta told her that no one knew what the letter said.

She told Goldie it was from Ms. Bland. Gwenetta was getting ready to say something else, but Drake had come over and touched Gwenetta on the shoulder and shook his head from side to side. Gwenetta then proceeded to tell Goldie that Ms. Bland had told her when Goldie was only three years old to give her the envelope when she turned twenty-one years old. Regretably, they were not in contact with each other at that time. Gwenetta asked Goldie to forgive her for waiting so long to carry out Ms. Bland's instructions.

Goldie found herself thinking why Ms. Bland would have entrusted Gwenetta with this request. She slowly turned and walked back to the couch. Gwenetta and Drake excused themselves. They stated that they felt Goldie needed to be alone as she read the letter inside the envelope. Goldie was also carrying the large Bible with her. As she sat down, the Bible opened up to the family tree section. It appeared that this section had been well documented. She immediately spotted

Ms. Bland's name. As she allowed her finger to follow the branches, she discovered something that almost caused her scream out loud. There it was, Carnegie Louisa Johnson was the mother of Gwenetta Ryeissa Bland who was married to Charles Drake Monroe parents of Marigold Louisa Monroe. Just as she was trying to digest this bit of news, her eyes followed the tree branch from Ms Bland to Forrest Yetis York son of Willie Jake Johnson and Anna Blake.

What she found most interesting was that Willie Jake Johnson was also the father of Ms Bland, but her mother's name was Kristie Marshall Johnson. Goldie had decided that she needed to talk to Gwenetta, when the envelope fell to the floor as though reminding her to read its content. Her trembling hands managed to remove the letter that consisted of six pages. Ms. Bland's words were very personable. It was as though she was speaking directly to Goldie.

"No doubt you have established your on life by now my Dearest Sweet Goldie. I see only good things in your future. I hope that you are not distressed by having to humor an old absent lady in your young adult years. I developed a strong attachment to you the first time I saw you in your mother's arms. Your beautiful brown eyes mesmerized me. Your innocent charm turned out to be your strongest asset. You were a child in control. I could feel your energy. I hoped I would live to see you through your teenage years, but when you turned three, I was diagnosed with a terminal illness. The doctors gave me a year to live, but they did not know I had a secret elixir that would give me three more years of joy and happiness. You became my closest companion. After my husband died, I dreaded waking up every day. However, when Gwenetta and Drake agreed to have me move near them so I could get to know my soon to be born granddaughter (yes, I said grandaughter) I was simply elated. Why the deception, your parents will have to answer that. As for the purpose of this letter, it has to do with a matter of inheritance. I want you to know that I have divided my estate into three divisions. You, Gwenetta and Yetis are my three closest surviving heirs. I do not know what has been shared with you about your family's history. I will tell you that I was an only child for the first fifteen years of my life. When I turned fifteen, it was rumored that my father had a son. He denied this. My father was a Baptist minister and well respected in the community. He could not and would not own up to the fact that he had an outside child. The woman who made the claim was a school teacher. She lost her job after the rumor circulated that my father was being named in the maternity suit. Somehow my father was able to contest it and win. The woman moved way after the child was born leaving him to be raised by her mother and an uncle. My dear mother however, told me it was true that my father was also the boy's father and she wanted me to make some kind of connection with my brother. Unfortunately, my mother died at the age of fifty-eight before father who lived to be seventy-eight years old. I had to wait until father's death to make contact with my brother. This brother is married to your father's sister. Perhaps by now you have met my brother, who is affectionately called Yetis. My father left everything to me when he died. I was able to give Yetis some of the money that I inherited at that time. He was thirty-three years old, married and had two sons. Your inheritance is to be made available to you when you turn twenty-five years old. Your mother's inheritance is to be given to her at the time of my death. I also have left some additional funds for Yetis. The family Bible is also being given to you. Please continue to record the family history in it. I have a cousin Jessie Gray who is living in Harahan. Please contact her. She and her husband Harold Gray can give you more details about my mother's side of the family. With love, hugs and kisses, Your grandmother, Carnegie Louisa Johnson Bland.

Goldie found herself reading the letter over and over again. It is a small world after all she thought. She looked up and saw Bomar walking toward her. He sat down beside her and put his arm around her. She looked searchingly into his eyes. Then she realized he knew. Of course, Uncle Yetis had told him. She concluded everybody knew.

As Bomar entered the room, he broke the silence by asking her if she was alright. Without waiting for an answer, he embraced her tighter. Goldie was beginning to feel a calm come over her. She just wanted to remain in Bomar's embrace. She had almost forgotten how that man had made her feel so sensual, so complete, so safe and so loved.

This calming moment was suddenly, broken by the loud and piercing scream of a female's voice. Goldie jumped up. She recognized that voice as belonging to Dakota. What could have caused her friend to be so disturbed? Was she determined to wake up even the dead? Goldie felt immobilized as Dakota continued screaming. Bomar told her to remain in the living room. He dashed out. Goldie watched as all of the other occupants of the house rush to the stairs. Dakota was no longer screaming, but she was crying "No! No! It can't be!" very emphatically. Goldie also thought she was hearing Greer screaming, "Call Dr. Madison!"

She could not stand still any longer. She rushed up the stairs, passing Gwenetta in her wheel chair sobbing uncontrollably. As she made it to the top of the stairs, she saw everybody was gathered in her aunt and uncle's bedroom. She slowly entered the room trying not to look at the faces of the occupants. Caleb and Greer, stepped back to allow her to get closer to the bed. Goldie stared at her aunt looking so peaceful. She appeared to have a slight smile on her face. Her right arm was positioned across her chest. She appeared to be clenching something in her right hand. She still had on her night gown. Goldie found herself looking toward her closet. There on the door hung her aunt's yellow golden smock. Goldie found herself going limp. Then she fainted.

Goldie awoke a few hours later. Dakota had to fill her in on the details of what happened after she fainted. Doctor Madison had rushed in within seconds of Goldie fainting. He gave her a small sedative after pronouncing Aunt Soya as having gone to Glory. He had the nurse who had come with him call for an ambulance. Then Bomar and Caleb carried Goldie to her room.

"What time is it?" She managed to ask Dakota.

"It's about 08:15 p.m."

"What time did Dr. Madison say Aunt Soya passed?"

"He estimated the time to be around 5 a.m. to 6 a. m."

"Dakota, will you help me get out of bed. I need to go to Aunt Soya's room."

"Aunt Soya is gone, Goldie. The ambulance arrived within 15 minutes after you fainted."

"Dakota, I need to check on something in my aunt's closet. Is everybody else down stairs?"

"I think so, but I am not sure if you should be walking around until you eat something. You became delirious when Dr. Madison gave you that sedative. I've been sitting here listening to you talk as though Aunt Soya was in the room with you. You keep repeating something about a chest in the closet and telling Uncle Yetis that you love him."

Suddenly, Bomar entered the room accompanied by a handsome stranger who he introduced as Napoleon Hart. Dakota realized he was Goldie's friend from work. Aunt Soya had told her about him. She immediately felt an attraction toward Napoleon which surprised her. They wanted to know if Goldie was awake and ready for some company. She said yes and quickly excused herself. She felt awkward in Napoleon's presence.

Goldie was glad Dakota left the room. She felt Bomar would accompany her to her aunt's room without asking a lot of questions. Both he and Napoleon agreed to do so. Upon entering the room, Goldie was perturbed to see that the beddings had been completely removed. She hesitated momentarily. Then, she saw the yellow smock still hanging on the closet door. Bomar suggested that she should come back later. She insisted on staying. She walked over to the smock and touched it with both hands. She felt that she was regaining her composure. She asked Bomar to open the closet door and look on the floor in the left corner for a wooden chest. Bomar located the chest and pulled it out. Goldie knelt down and lifted the lid up to see the contents. The first thing that she saw was a sealed 11x14 envelop with the single word "Will" written on it. Beneath it was her doll, CanCan. She could not believe her aunt kept the doll for her. The doll was lying on top of a photo album and more important looking papers. She stood up holding both the doll and the will in her hand. She asked Bomar to bring the chest to her bedroom. Naopoleon helped escort her back to her bedroom.

Goldie decided to sit in a chair when she returned to her room. Bomar put the chest on the floor beside her. She asked him and Napoleon to have a seat in the two extra chairs that had been brought into the room. She held CanCan in her arms like a little girl.

Napoleon was very concerned about the frame of mind of his dear young friend. Bomar had filled him in on as much as he could upon his arrival. After a few more moments of silence, he cleared his throat to speak. "Goldie, I already informed Mr. Drummaday about the passing of Aunt Soya. He sends his condolences and he said take all the extra time that you need to take care of matters. I hopped on the fastest flight that I could to be with you. I will, however, be flying back tomorrow night on a 9:30 flight. Caleb has insisted that I spend the night here. My mother and aunts send their love." Napoleon got up out of his seat and leaned over to kiss Goldie on the forehead. "I am going to leave you here with Bomar and I am going to ask Dakota to bring you a cup of warm spicy tea that I will be preparing. My mother insisted that I bring the tea to give you energy. I love you, my little darling." Napoleon told Bomar to watch Goldie closely as he left the room.

Bomar watched in silence as Napoleon left the room. Then he turned his attention toward Goldie. He remained quiet for several minutes. He wanted so much to comfort her. Finally, he decided he needed to speak. "Your friend, Napoleon is very impressive. I am relieved that he did not pursue you for himself."

Bomar spoke with mocked jealousy. Goldie had not said a word since they returned to her room. She did manage a smile and he thought how youthful and beautiful she looked sitting in the chair holding her doll. He was determined not to let her out of his life no matter what changes he would have to make. He looked at the clock radio. The time was 9:45 p.m. "Goldie, he said almost in a whisper, "I hope my timing is not offensive to you. However, your Uncle Yetis always told me to seize the moment. When you first stumbled into my life, I wanted you so desperately. Unfortunately, I withheld the truth about my marriage from you. I was afraid that you would not be able to deal with that. I realize now that reaching out to someone is about revealing who you really are. For me, that was not an easy thing to do. New relationships can be compared to two blind individuals touching, clutching, and feeling each other all over. There is an implied need to want to know everything about the other person. Please understand, Goldie, the intense love and passion that I felt for you were genuine. Now I need you more than ever to be in my life so that I can continue on with my life. I have come full circle, Goldie. I had a lot of growing to do. I do not want you to complete me. I want you to unite with me. I see a more mature Goldie. I guess things happen for a reason. I believe we have both grown full circle. Together we can be empowered to grow in love and trust. This time I can honestly ask you from the beginning to be my life partner. I have already asked Napoleon to be my best man."

"Suddenly, a loud screamed ranged out. It was Dakota, again. This time it was a joyful cry. She was shouting, "Say yes, girlfriend. Yes! Yes! Yes!" Of course, her screaming caused the other household members to rush up the stairs again. Apparently, Dakota had returned to bring Goldie her cup of tea.

Goldie and Bomar had been unaware of her presence outside the door. She had listened quietly as Bomar poured out his heart to Goldie. As Caleb and Greer rushed past her into the room, she started jumping up down. She had placed the tray holding the tea on the floor outside of the door. When Caleb saw that Goldie was alright, they turned to Dakota. By now, Napoleon had also made his way back up the stairs. Drake and Gweneta remained at the foot of the stairs. Dakota skipped towards the stairs and made her way down softly singing, "There's going to be a wedding. There's going to be a wedding. Oh, how wonderful. There's going to be a wedding!"

Goldie was amused by Dakota's dramatic response to a scene that should have been private. But that was so typical of Dakota. Bomar was still waiting on a response from her. She looked lovingly at him and smiled. Then she said, "Yes, there is going to be a wedding right here in Harahan." Before he could grab Goldie, Caleb and Greer were in front of him. Greer lifted her up from the chair. Caleb turned to Bomar and grabbed his hand. Napoleon was grabbing for his hand as well saying congratulations. Goldie kept telling Greer to put her down. Instead, he carried her out of the room and down the stairs. The others followed. Drake and Gwenetta surmised that her answer must have been yes. When Greer finally put her down next to Bomar, Goldie looked around at all of them. She thought how fortunate that she was at last to be surrounded by all of the people who were dearest to her. In the back of them, she thought for a moment that she saw Aunt Soya and Uncle Yetis enter the room smiling and waving at her. She smiled and waved back causing the others to turn around. The front door was slightly ajar. Caleb went to close it and winked at Goldie.

Suddenly Dakota commented out loud, "What color will I be wearing to the wedding?"

Caleb quickly responded, "Just do not wear all black. A wedding is a new beginning and you will be joining in to quote my father, "the celebration of a self—rising flower." Be nice, young lady!"

Everyone burst into laughter, including Dakota.

As Goldie prepared for bed that night, she noticed the time was 11:45 p.m. She decided this was definitely the "Eve of her Good Night." Learning about the dynamics of her family's history had been cathartic. As she felled into REM sleep, she felt as though she was being energized. She was experiencing surround sound. She was visualizing with clarity the faces of Ms. Carnegie, Uncle Yetis and Aunt Soya. They were providing her with channels of love. She was a self—rising flower rising ever higher. She was running barefooted on the sandy beech at sunset. It was her golden hour. She could see waves emitting vibrant colors. They rose up high and came crashing down and splashed their sparkling waters as though saluting the stars. It was riotous. Uncle Yetis was right. The truth had indeed surfaced even stronger.